# leaving
# las vegas

# john
# o'brien

# leaving
# las vegas
# john
# o'brien

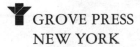

GROVE PRESS
NEW YORK

Copyright © 1990 by John O'Brien

All rights reserved. No part of this book may be reproduced in any form or by any electronic or mechanical means, including information storage and retrieval systems, without permission in writing from the publisher, except by a reviewer, who may quote brief passages in a review.

First published in 1990 by Watermark Press
First Grove Press paperback edition published in 1995

*Published simultaneously in Canada*
*Printed in the United States of America*

ISBN: 0-8021-3445-9

Library of Congress Catalog Card Number: 95-81572

Design by John Baxter

Grove Press
841 Broadway
New York, NY 10003

10 9 8 7 6 5 4

*For Lisa,*
*close to the action*

# leaving
# las vegas

# john
# o'brien

cherries

Sucking weak coffee
plastic lid of a red and
Sera spots a place to s

# hrough a hole in the green styrofoam cup, t down. She has been

walking around now for at least two hours and wants desperately to rest. Normally she wouldn't dare hang around this long in front of a 7-11, but the curb looks high and, having recently accumulated a fresh coat of red paint, not too dirty. She drops down hard on the cold curb and hugs her knees, bending her head into the privacy of the dark little cave created by her arms. Her eyes follow the stream of light running between her two thighs, down to where it concludes in black lace, aptly exposed by her short leather skirt.

She throws back her head, and her dark brown hair fans around her shoulders, dances in the turbulence created by a passing Sun Bus; a window framed profile begins to turn and vanishes in a cloud of black exhaust. In the red gloss of her recently applied lipstick there is a tiny reflection of the glowing convenience store sign, its cold fluorescent light shining much too white to tan or warm the beautiful face appealing beneath it. She modestly lowers her knees, only to have the black blazer fall open as she leans back on her elbows, revealing her small breasts under a sheer lace camisole. Making no effort to cover herself, she turns her head; her dark green eyes, protected by long mascara-laden lashes, scan up and down Las Vegas Boulevard.

*Tadatadatacheeda tacheek tacheek sheeka* she catches on her lips an unrefined tune, already in progress. All but inaudible, composed clumsily out of fragments overheard in casino lounges, it nonetheless seems to guide the passing traffic, coercing the rumble and whine of the street to perform in symphony with the slide and twirl that exist in her head. Across the street—not yet over the shiver, nor to the goods—a dormant construction site, populated with skeletal cranes raising adolescent towers, stands smugly, silently, and in dubious approval. It wears the green and blue hues of the night. It knows not whence it came. It will lend her the benefit of the doubt. It will accompany her on the long, hard, painful ride in a car filled with chums. Sera's arms are weak, but her pulse is strong. She smacks shut her lips and waits for a trick.

The warm air gusts through an invisible maze. Sera watches little dust tornadoes rise and fall, pieces of litter riding on the currents. She finds in her purse a foil-wrapped towelette, salvaged from some now forgotten fast-food meal. Opening it, she discreetly reaches under her camisole and wipes her breasts, then the back of her neck. Looming in the distance is a hill, or mountain, or some such overrated nonsense.

She watches as a staggering drunk, heading east on the near sidewalk, takes a dive directly in front of her. He lies motionless, and Sera, slightly concerned, calls to him.

"Hey! Are you alive?" she says.

He doesn't respond, and she knows that he's probably just passed out and that now she'll have to move before the police come and pick him up.

She tries again. "Hey, you better get up before the cops come. You want me to help you?"

He groans out what sounds like *no* and starts to move. Feeling embarrassed for him she looks away, and when she looks back, after scanning the street for heat, he is gone.

His point was made, and he moved along, in keeping with the tangential nature that must consume at least one of them. There is a bottle in his future—perhaps sooner a glass—elsewhere on the line. Sera is a circle, twenty-nine years around.

Once a small girl in the east, she now lives here. There was time spent in Los Angeles, but the story that she knows is working well here, working at its best here, and she wishes to stay here in Las Vegas, where she arrived long enough ago that she now calls it home when speaking with herself. Her perspicacity intact— indeed, augmented by the rough spots—she came here deliberately and hewed out a life on her own terms which happens to fit quite nicely with local hustle-bustle policies. The tough, desperate life of the fictional prostitute, if she ever really knew it, is now long behind her; the tough is in fact manageable; the desperate turned out to be a not-very exclusive club. In any case, she can handle it, all of it. There will always be dark characters, but her life is good; it is as she wishes it to be.

She can bring the most out of most of the men that she *does;* this is the hardest part, but it is also the best part. Unsuspecting, they are distracted by their imminent ejaculations and rarely realize that they have let slip some tiny communication, some clue to their identity, some test of themselves. Sera is far away from the well-known, overblown and arbitrary definitions of what accomplishment is. She *sees* these guys while they're fucking her. Sometimes she *talks* to these guys. *Some*times these guys *talk* to her. This is a good thing.

She stands and walks to a trash can with her soiled towelette, pausing along the way to pick up a discarded piece of cellophane, de-Twinkied and blowing across the 7-11 parking lot.

And she is a good thing, good at this thing. Paying for and using her, there are always men available. The tricks turn to her, for she glistens with the appealing inaccessibility of the always introspective. They turn to the buyable quench—no lie, a promise in the panties—and she plays out the bargain with the competence of one consistently able to hit well the mark. No matter how long it has been since she last worked, she is never without a full arsenal of idiosyncratic performances, ready in an instant to fall into the groove and take command without missing a beat. Her tricks go away quietly, their burden of dissatisfaction lessened sufficiently to fulfill the terms of any implied agreement that may have been struck.

The men that come to her are varied in appearance as well as disposition, though most share a few common denominators. They all are able to define a need and then take steps to satisfy it. Not lost in self-doubt over their masculinity, either at terms with it or indifferent to it, they come to and effect the logical connection between lust and money. They can translate one hundred dollars into thirty minutes of renting a female body, and they perceive this translation exactly as it is: a piece of commerce, not a profound commentary. Many are seeking fuel for masturbation, a highlight in the cycle, tangible experience on which to outline the fantasy. These men all find delight in the opportunity to relate to a woman on sexual terms with complete candor. Leaving at home all the potential drawbacks of the sex act—many their own doing—they are now in a clean environment where you ask for something and either get it or don't, without putting at risk the whole circumstance. They are maintaining. They are maximizing solution and minimizing difficulty. They have generally similar, specifically different, reasons for seeing her. Sera turns and walks to the street, to the slowing car, to the greeting, to the initial rap.

Cued by the fall of the power window, she leans to the car. She is not in, not even near the car, but with the flair of an illusionist she has the driver believing she is very close indeed. The perennial tingle in her tummy, a smile of measured insouciance, then: "Hi!" He'll be okay. He's about fifty, a little nervous, a regular bather, rather unattractive but with affable eyes. She tilts her head, catches in the rear window the red and green reflection of the convenience store sign, and says with an unprofessional giggle, "Were you looking to spend some time, or are you just here for a Slurpee?"

Managing a smile—though this is clearly not what he expected—he says, "Well... yes. How much is a... Slurpee?" With this a twitch and a wider grin: trying to play along.

Sera, deciding to abandon the metaphor before it gets too precious, presses her lips together appraisingly and whispers with a teenage wink, "One hundred. One hour max at... what hotel?"

He gives her the name of a rather well-known and gaudy establishment, brightening at the opportunity to invoke it, and Sera could have almost mouthed the name simultaneously. He coughs, slightly uncomfortable again, and asks, "What's... umm, what's included? I mean, what will you do?"

"Well, unless I miss my guess, I should be able to do just about anything you're inclined to ask for." Realizing that they're spending too much time in such an overt situation, she looks around quickly and says confidentially, "We'd better work this out pretty quick."

"Ninety dollars," he blurts out: a real pro.

She likes him, gives him an *A* for effort. "Fine. Then you'll be happy to hear that I've got change for a hundred."

He reaches over and pushes the car door open. Sera climbs in, and before reaching the hotel they manage to discuss prostitution, black girls, and his children—in that order. One block down from the 7-11, in a yellow Mercedes, which is parked in the shadow of a silver camper and bears expired British Columbian plates, sits a sallow-skinned man, cutting a lone figure indeed.

On the eleventh floor of her trick's hotel, having survived a misdirected march resulting from a wrong turn off the elevator, Sera lies on a surprisingly lumpy mattress and feels the familiar friction in her vagina. She stares at the ceiling, vaguely preoccupied despite herself, unable to give her full attention to the middle-aged man who is pumping away on top of her, but also aware that his is not the sort that would notice or care. He'll come in a couple of minutes, then hurriedly whisk her from his night. Practical, not overly abusive, his type is her bread and butter. Though she did blush, momentarily and despite herself, when in his car he remarked of her beauty and smiled for her.

She is thinking, as his freckled shoulder nudges rhythmically against her chin, of another trick that she turned years ago, on the corner of Sunset and Western in Los Angeles. (He was quiet and polite, and they quickly came to an agreement. She waited as he parked his car then took him down the block to a house that she had access to and which was kept for such purposes. Upon entering what would have been the living room, she instructed him to give twenty dollars to the fat Mexican sitting on the couch watching television. He did and the Mexican pointed to an open door next to an empty crib behind them. Sera led the man to the assigned room, carefully stepping around the four or five infants that crawled on the dirty carpet, crying and in various states of undress. The room contained a dresser and, surprisingly, an actual bed, not just a cot. Having tucked away her newest hundred dollar bill, she undressed. He had already taken a position lying on his back, so she put the rubber on him and, after sucking him for a few minutes, eased herself onto him. Twenty minutes later the time knock sounded on the door and he still hadn't come. Sera felt somehow guilty and offered to secure ten more minutes, but he thanked her and refused. He had hardly spoken a word the whole time, and after he was dressed, she let him hug her and kiss her cheek. He tipped her with another hundred and went back to his car. Ultimately she was glad to have the extra money, as she really didn't feel like working for some time after that.)

The man ejaculates, gripping the mattress with one tense, white fist, Sera with the other. He rolls off of her and lies still, waiting for the turmoil to settle in his body, precious few years away, she guesses, from the time when moments like this will produce in him secret fears, imagined pains in his arm and chest. Sera, older and more weary than she was in Hollywood, still living in a world that plays in a time window not yet sullied by death-sentence venereal diseases, only occasionally insists on a rubber, relying on her judgment, experience, and instinct to tell her when. She reaches for a nearby towel and holds it between her legs as she walks to the bathroom. She cleans, dresses, says goodbye before shutting the door.

She smiles at her reflection in a polished copper panel until, fully descended, the elevator doors open to the perennial cacophony of the casino. There is a poetry to this noise, and Sera has yet to tire of it. She looks her part; anyhow, the real mistakes are made in the larger rooms. So it is that a steel-eyed man with long and oft manicured fingernails blocks her path with his well-fed bulk and holds up two black disks. One hundred dollar chips,

these, held each in its own well-kept hand, speciously and between their noses as if they were tokens of hypnosis. Disregarding
passers by, he slowly lowers the chips and presses them against
Sera's chest, one each on the tips of her breasts. A wry grin on her
face, she follows his hands with her eyes and continues to stare at
them until the moment becomes protracted and uncomfortable.

"What's the problem?" says the man, dropping his hands.
"You on strike?" This amuses him, and he walks away laughing
loudly, so as to confirm to anyone who might be watching that it
was he who commanded the situation all along.

(She couldn't help it. He had bought them all that beer, and
she had had more than her share. But it didn't help, 'cause when
her turn came she was so nervous that she peed right on his hand.
He got mad and looked like he was gonna hit her, but he didn't.

He stopped and looked around at them, all her girlfriends
laughing at him, and he took his hand out of his own pants and
walked back to the clearing in the front of the park. Sera was sorry
to have ruined things, sorrier still about the look on his face as he
left, like he had just gotten beat up.)

"Aren't you a cute little trick," says another good-natured,
lecherous cab driver to Sera as she falls into his backseat. He chats
about his last fare and takes her back to the part of the Strip that
she likes to work.

She, feeling pretty good about finding herself in yet another
harmless evening, chats back freely. This is standard fare, replete
with the simple details of breathing and talking, of tasting and
swallowing, of washing and drying, of watching and defining. She
can and will do this forever. Rare in her race, rarer still in her
class, she touches—even now—the things that others only grasp
for futilely at the instant of unavailability. Her grass is very green
indeed.

And to it she returns as she rises from the cab and glances

down the street, only to glimpse the same yellow Mercedes that she noticed earlier. The car backs quickly out of view, leaving behind the urgent echo of hot rubber on pavement and a protesting horn amidst the waning scream of internal combustion.

This is bad news at best, for she once knew a man with a penchant for Mercedes and a proclivity for amateur surveillance, a man lurking in her past, lurking, hopefully, elsewhere. There is only one other girl in sight, and she was not here earlier, nor does she appear very attentive now. Furthermore, as far as Sera can tell only one thing happened immediately prior to the car's hasty departure, and that was her obvious sighting of it.

She settles on one more look at the empty space next to the silver camper, and relegating the matter to the back of her mind, she turns her attention back to the business at hand. After all, this Mercedes—this *yellow* Mercedes—is not quite in the same league with the very expensive, very tacky, gold-plated German chariots in her past, and it is not at all unusual for girls working the Strip to be watched for hours by nervous men or cheap-thrill masturbators.

("This is what you are, Sera! This is what I say you are!"

She waited, almost hungrily, for the blade, the metal that would go into her flesh then be in her flesh. She wanted it, perhaps, because her experience had taught her that that which begins will also end. Face down, she bit the pillow.

"Sera!" he cried. He was crying now. There were tears.

But she preferred to concentrate on the sensation of warm, flowing blood. It seemed the simpler of the two fluids.)

The Strip is swinging up, acting up as the midwesterners embrace their newly found early a.m. options. Sera really has no immediate need to be here, as she has earned enough already tonight for a full day at the tables tomorrow, but working full-time has become a sort of habit for her, and she just doesn't feel right when she goes home much before two in the morning. She decides that she's about one trick away from her morning shower, just as three college boys, each wearing numbered jerseys and carrying the ubiquitous Heineken bottles, walk toward her from the street.

"How much will it cost us to fuck you?" says the tallest, amidst the titters of the other two. His shirt bears the number sixteen—his age minus three, she guesses.

Sera starts to turn away, then pauses to button her blazer. "Sorry guys, but I don't know what you mean. Anyway, I never date more than one guy at a time," she says.

"Come on, we got money. Show her the money, Mike," says sixteen. Both hands firmly entrenched in his back pockets, he gestures with his chin to his comrade.

Number twelve opens his wallet to her, exposing several hundred of what she knows are daddy's poorly-placed dollars. Of course it's possible that this little episode is exactly what daddy had in mind: *Where's your son, Frank?*—chuckles from around the club locker room—*Why hell, Charlie, I sent 'im off to Vegas to learn the one thing I couldn't teach 'im!*. She realizes it's a bad idea, but she bites just the same.

She clucks her tongue: the disapproving mother. "How much of that did you guys want to spend?" she says.

Sixteen brightens visibly, but catches himself; his earlier boasting has not embarrassed him as he feared it might when they actually came up with the money. All business: "How much you want? How about two hundred for an hour?" he says: not my money.

"Don't your friends talk?" she says, growing annoyed, despite herself, with this kid's presumption. This is not a good idea; they'll end up disliking her, probably mistreat hundreds of women down the road because of her. "Try three hundred for a half-hour."

"Three hundred for an hour," says double zero, grasping the next logical step as he speaks for the first time. Mistake. Though her manner has put him at ease he can hear a quiver in his own voice, and he resolves not to speak anymore.

"Three hundred and we'll see how it goes," says Sera, wondering if they could possibly all be virgins. Certainly one of them is, and she bets that this is some sort of ritual for his benefit.

They all nod and twelve starts to count out the money to her with a certain dejected resolution. He hadn't expected this to go so well, and hoping to be absolved from all responsibility by the older boy's leadership, he had other plans for these crisp bills.

She stops him with a gesture. "Where's your room, what hotel?" she asks.

They tell her, and it turns out to be a little motel, not far from where they are. Not exactly top security for her, but she just can't muster a rational doubt about this trick. Anyway, they're all impressed with their friend now—he's so well-bonded that he's practically glowing—and she would hate to let them down.

"I'll see you there in fifteen minutes," she says. "You can pay me then. Why don't you all take a shower while you're waiting."

"In fifteen minutes?" whines twelve.

"Don't you guys live in a dorm or something? You must have some experience with quick showers, right? Didn't you ever have two dates in one night?"—everybody's all smiles now—"Look, I'll only need one of you at a time, RIGHT? UNDERSTOOD?"— nods all around—"Well then, the other two can shower while I'm there." She snaps her lips shut and stares at them: end of conversation.

They walk off giggling. Sera goes into the store and buys a bottle of beer to help her decide whether or not she really wants to go through with this, but she arrives on time at their door and sixteen opens up in his Jockey shorts. She feels the tension as she goes into the room and is about to leave when twelve pushes the three hundred dollars at her. Against her better judgment, she stays, and starts undressing as double zero emerges from the bathroom, looking rather pale.

"Who's first?" she says.

(Of all the girls, she always went out first. Once she came back and they were all still there, watching TV, laughing, some of them fucking.

"It's because I love you the most," he said, "that I allow you to work the hardest.")

The boys look around at each other and at her. She doesn't want to think that they're checking relative positions, but she's been in similar scenes before. She still can't believe that these guys are dangerous.

"I want to fuck her in the butt, Jim." says twelve, looking hopefully at Jim. "You too, right?"

"Forget that," she says. "No one's doing that. You'll all go straight, one at a time. If you want I'll suck you instead, but that's all. Then I'm out of here." Yes, now it moves fast. I can feel it getting fast in here, she thinks.

"Jim, you said I could fuck her in the butt," repeats twelve.

"That's it, I'm leaving," she says. "Here's your money back." She picks up her purse.

"No! Stay," says Jim. "Shut up, Mike!"

"It's my money and I want to fuck her in the butt, Jim!" screams Mike.

She turns on him. "Maybe you want to fuck JIM in the butt! Have you thought of that?" she says.

Then, as she will remember it later, the scene begins moving *really* fast—way too fast to even think about fast—or perhaps it

simply compresses, crystallizes into a complex moment of images. Her challenge brings the room to silence, and she sees that
the boy's eyes are filling up with tears. Feeling bad, she tries to
apologize, but is stopped by a blow, catching her full in the face.
A flash of colored sparks lead her into darkness, unconscious-
ness. She wakes hurting, her face in a bloody pillow and someone
on her back. A scream and struggle bring only a glimpse of the tall
one—Jim... his name is Jim—in his underwear, then more
darkness. Sounds and cries come to her ears as she fades in and
out between blows. "Go on! fuck her!"... "Fuck her in the rear!"...
"Can we go home now?"... "Look at me, I'm fucking on her!" Hot
semen falls on her back, but she is too sore to know for sure if she
is being violated at any given moment. She hears someone
throwing up, and as she turns to look her hair is tugged hard,
snapping her head back and exposing her face to another punch.
"Stop that puking, Bobby."... "What's she gonna do, call the
cops?"... "This is what she does for a living."... "Don't worry,
she'll be fine." She is rolled over, wakes to see two of them
urinating on her breasts, and is kicked sharply on the side of her
head. There is a final flash of sparks, and she goes under, way, way
under.

♣   ♣   ♣

She bleeds freely, asleep on the well-bleached sheets, alone in the
little room.

(They were just boys, unwittingly paving their lives with
misery.)

A passing truck grinds by outside of the quiet room, its low
rumble entering her dormant ears and echoing unnaturally inside
her head.

(The bars were covered with blood and spit. The cop's hand

slipped off the iron rail as he rose from her, and the girls in the lockup pretended to rush him. They mocked his panic as he bolted, his pants still around his ankles. She saw other cops laughing, and wondered if he would ever live it down.)

*Ooooooommmmmmmmaaaaaaaa,* the sound oozes to the front of her head, first in a dream; then she almost knows it's a real sound, and she starts to pry her eyes open.

(Sera could tell, just by looking across the circular bar at them, that the expensive West Hollywood call girls had no time for her, and probably wished she wasn't around.)

The room is incandescent yellow at first, then white, altered by her mind as it recaptures awareness and strives for normalcy.

(They were afraid, afraid to be with her and with each other. Their bodies moved too fast for their brains to keep up.)

The pain knows that she is finally awake, and starts to assault her from all directions. Quivering, she pulls on her clothes. She knows that they won't be back, and ignores an impulse to run from the room. She guesses that she has been sodomized more than once, and each step to the mirror brings tears to her eyes as the pain rips through her. She wipes the blood and makeup from her swollen face, realizing that she won't be able to work for at least a week. She hopes that she can do well at the tables today, for a change. Finding her purse intact, she calls for a cab from the room phone; it arrives, and Sera, with visible difficulty, opens the door and sits gently on the bench seat.

"What's the matter honey, get a delivery at the back door that you weren't expectin'?" says the driver, laughing at her discomfort. He's a veteran, seen it all. Long ago, dues paid, he dispensed with his obligation to be courteous; never even had the inclination—*goes with the territory,* he tells the new guys. He goes with the territory. "Looks like you been knocked around, too. You got any money left? You gonna be able to pay your fare?"

She silently pulls a twenty dollar bill out of her purse and, reaching forward, drops it on the front seat.

"Oh, don't wanna talk to me?" he says, offended. "Well don't take it out on me, I'm just tryin' to cover my ass. What the hell do you expect sluttin' around like that, dressed like that? What the hell do you expect? You just oughtta be glad the creep didn't nail you the way I would. At least the way you got it you know you ain't knocked up. You oughtta be glad, that's all. Where you goin to?"

She mumbles her address through swollen lips.

"Fine," he says, easing up. "That's fine, and you'll have change comin'. How's that? See, it's not so bad. Hell, I didn't mean to laugh at ya, but you should have seen the way you sat down: like it was on eggs. I'm sorry you got hit, but you oughtta be glad cause it could be worse. I've seen worse. But this is fine, you got change comin' and you could be worse. See, I'm not such a bad guy. Now this is fine, okay? Whaddeya say?"

"Yeah," says Sera, "I'm fine. Thanks for asking. This is fine."

The cab zips by a tattered woman carrying two overloaded bags of laundry under the hot sun, several children in tow. Sera wonders at the woman's pain—or her ability to remain ignorant of it.

♣   ♣   ♣

The shade of the hotel tower has just crawled off of the yellow Mercedes; actually, it seemed to crawl slowly over the car and then dart quickly from the peripheral area, like a little girl who suddenly realizes that she is sitting next to a spider. The windows have been open all night, befitting the perpetual heat of the season. Taking advantage of the newly directed sunlight, the man in the car looks again into the cant rearview mirror at the image of a solitary gold chain, nestled in and somehow at home amidst his voluminous chest hair and unruly neck hair. He nods—an internal debate apparently resolved—and removes a second gold ring from his left pinky. There are now no rings on his left hand.

There is, however, a single, heavily-jeweled ring remaining on his right hand—the index finger—and this is the hand that now, shaking almost imperceptibly, holds the plastic handle of a disposable razor. It scrapes dryly across his face, making an unpleasant noise until one of the hotel's maintenance vehicles, brushes swirling, goes to work on a nearby area of the parking lot and drowns it out.

♣   ♣   ♣

Passing the green and gray pebble lawn in front of the one-story apartment building, small change in the cab forgotten, Sera swings open the security gate and limps toward her door, distinguished from the others by a once black, now faded gray italic 6, permanently affixed and reaffixed to the veneer with various nails and small screws. Inside she shuts the door and feels, as she always does when first entering her apartment, both relieved and threatened by the surprising silence of her home, a silence somehow augmented by the low bombilation of central air and frost-free refrigeration. She puts down her purse and sheds her clothing as she hobbles about, restoring each belonging to its proper location in the appropriate room or closet, maintaining an orderly state of affairs. Herself finally naked and placed in the shower stall, she rotates the chrome knobs and releases the water, standing braced under the spray until her trembling knees fail and she collapses onto the tile wall in front of her; gripping the porcelain soap dish, she feels the water beat on her back and watches it disappear down the drain.

(Even the black girls were constantly hassled. The outcalls, the houses, everybody was in the path of The Policy Cops and their pervasive attempts to piss off the Very Bad Guys. The only girls left working—other than those in the Korean houses—were the desperate junkies. For Sera the problems were even more critical, more personal. She was haunted, pursued, tortured emotionally, sometimes physically, day and night by the one who had made her the object of his obsession. She was and would become his last, best gold chain, an unwilling bauble on his furry chest. He had made it just too hard for her to stay in Los Angeles, so three years after arriving from the East, she had to move, had to leave the little life that she had built.)

Spanking clean, she dries herself with two towels and walks tiptoe over the cold tile floor out of the bathroom and into her bed. As each muscle settles into temporary disuse, her mind, now entrusting control of her body to the soft bed, accelerates, reviewing the day, the week, the month—all the sublimity, all the poetically prosaic moments of her deliberate life—until it abruptly stops and, with the easy effort of survival, drops Sera and her past into a dreamless sleep.

♣　♣　♣

Far outside of town on the way to Henderson there are four or five pawn shops littering the highway. In front of one of these is parked the yellow Mercedes, its owner waiting for the passing of a highway patrol car that might object to expired Canadian license plates. He has driven this distance to avoid being spotted at a pawn shop by anyone who may know him, but in truth there is almost no one who knows him.

The air is hot and dry, and though this man is genetically built for such a climate, these days he is not properly wound for his environment, or perhaps he is simply naked for the first time. At least now he has some money in his pocket, fewer rings on his fingers.

♣　♣　♣

Sera awakens roughly seven hours later to the early evening sounds of her neighbors returning home from their jobs. She turns to look at the clock and then stops before seeing it, remembering that, with her face beaten, she has no schedule of her own to keep, and with its disregard for hours, Las Vegas has none to impose upon her. Resisting a second impulse to look at the time, she gets up instead to urinate.

At the bathroom sink she peers into the mirror and examines the current version of her look. She has, on the right side of her face, two distinct multicolor bruises, one each in the areas of her eye and cheek, the latter extending inward to swollen lips and upward to her nose, where, compounded by the swell of the former, it transforms her once and future beauty into quite an asymmetrical event. Certainly it's been worse, perhaps will be again. The pain is really only as bad as the time spent on it, and apart from the dull throbbing ache, punctuated by occasional sharp stings of pain, she feels mostly irritation at the inconvenience. Not that she didn't walk into it, almost ask for it by ignoring her gut feeling, but she has always tried so hard to play by all the rules, and she feels that in exchange for this acquiescence she should be allowed to proceed unmolested to conclusion. Or, if that is not quite right, at least she knows that she is as hard as she's going to get and has been for a long time. Glaring at herself, she waits for her vexation to pass, knowing that it has no more basis than its cause. Nothing has changed; there is no toll to be collected, no psychological scar to flaunt. The world is evidently about to let her stick around: good deal, she knows. She also knows that this episode is now, physical evidence to the contrary, pretty much over. She goes to the television and turns on the evening news. In the kitchen she makes a pot of coffee, puts some bread in the toaster.

Fed, feeling better, still in possession—not surprisingly—of the three bills from last night's trick du jour—and then some— she brushes her teeth and hair, puts on her jeans and tee shirt and walks to the bus stop.

(Intentionally she stayed a step behind, hanging back in the bushes—the *woods* to neighborhood children, actually just a small grouping of trees in someone's backyard—not quite hiding deliberately enough so that she couldn't plausibly deny it should she be discovered. The yellow bus came and went, leaving her alone at the stop and gleeful at the success of her deception. She waited in the winter wind for the next bus, the *late kids'* bus, filled with not-so-familiar faces, kids that wouldn't know her so well, wouldn't know the mocking chants that stung her ears every other morning.)

She arrives downtown and makes a few passes up and down Fremont before strolling into one of the virtually interchangeable casinos in that area. Finding an empty five dollar table, meeting the resentful glare of the dealer, whose arms are folded in judgment and inactivity, she slips into the center seat and smooths a hundred out in front of her, rotating and casually examining it in mocking anticipation of the dealer's own predictable actions. He, the dealer, stands immobile; his only reaction is an annoyed "shuffle-up," which escapes his rigid lips without the benefit of even an insincere exclamation point. Sera knows this guy. All regular gamblers know this guy. He's the Las Vegas equivalent of the dour postal worker who's irked at the propagation of corre-

spondence in this country; except that there are many more angry
dealers per peer capita than there are angry postal workers. This
one is fanning out his cards in front of him, flips them over for a
moment: everyone can see. Various ritualistic machinations follow, to the point where she finds herself in temporary charge of
two green and ten red chips—these in exchange for her one
hundred dollars—and two cards—these in exchange for her
placing one of her red chips in the circle outlined on the green felt
in front of her. She and the dealer then spend about twenty
minutes swapping cards and chips back and forth without any
substantial or lasting exchange of wealth.

Sera is a competent player knowing all the right plays but has
never been serious enough to learn the memory mechanics of card
counting, a skill that would give her a slight advantage over the
house and therefore more or less consistent winnings during the
course of her habitual play. As it is she experiences only short
runs of good or bad luck, with the balance of her play blending
into a low profile blandness that seems to make the casinos happy
as they whittle away at her money until it is gone. Only then, her
leisure time completed, can she go home and prepare to earn
more, which will be willingly offered up, with full cognizance that
it is being sacrificed, when she sits again at the tables, in the
casinos, which are under the jurisdiction of the Nevada Gaming
Commission, which, small evidence to the contrary, has no
wisdom that hasn't long ago been gained by Sera.

A well-built man wearing a gold cross chained around his
neck, a moustache, and a cologne that he probably couldn't name,
nonchalantly sits down next to her and commences spraying her
with quick sideways glances and vulgar grins. He offers to buy
her a drink, and she points out that the casino would have already
done that had she wanted one.

"High roller?" he smirks, indicating her five dollar bet on the table. He adds a chip to his own bet, bringing it up to ten dollars. "There's a charm. My name's Stephen. Maybe I'll bring you luck, ____."

"Sera," she says. "Where are you visiting from?" *San Diego.*

They both stand against the dealer's four and lose to his drawn seven.

"Damn!" says Stephen. "I hate those damn unfair twenty-ones. Phoenix, Sarah. You?" He puts another ten dollars in his betting circle.

"They do seem unfair. Here," she says. She decides to bet ten also and notices that when she does he raises his bet to fifteen. "You can't bluff me, you know."—indicating with a nod his bet— "This isn't poker." She smiles.

"No," he says, smiling back at her smile, "really, Phoenix."

Nodding, this time to his response, she drops it and increases her bet to fifteen before the deal. He quickly raises his to twenty.

"What are you doing?" she says, indicating his bet.

"Just playing the game, Sarah," he says, and rubs the back of his neck with his left hand.

The dealer busts and they both win. Stephen watches Sera's bet before removing any of his own from the circle. She leaves her thirty dollars at risk. He adds ten to the forty already in front of him and then wipes his left hand on his pant leg. He is dealt a pair of fives against the dealer's ace: a good start, for it is a total of ten.

"It can't get much worse. Split 'em," he says, pulling out a fifty dollar bill from a large roll. He winks at her.

It just did, she thinks to herself without looking at his draw, knowing that his ineptitude has turned a solid hand into two bust cards.

"Money plays," says the dealer, placing the fifty next to Stephen's chips. For the first time he is attentive and almost enthused; he's eating this up.

"Why did you do that, Stephen?" she says when he loses both bets. "Hell, if you had to lose some money you would have at least been better off doubling!"

He mutters something about taking a chance and excuses himself from the table. He probably would have preferred losing ten times that amount to looking foolish in the eyes of a woman. Sera realizes that he committed no crime, feels bad, wishes she had kept quiet, wishes she would get better at identifying the moment.

("Maybe I didn't think that was so great... mmmebbie I want my money back," he said, making his hand into a fist theatrically up in the air so she could surely see it.

She watched him closely for a clue, but found none. Cursing her own indecision, she suddenly realized that his penis, still inside of her, was shrinking.

"Maybe you should fuck yourself next time. Get off me," she said. Though her heart was beating hard, pushing her better judgment frantically to her head, she kept her tone and manner solid, even a little bit bored and sounding aloof.

His gaze dropped an inch, then even he knew that he had lost, had betrayed himself. He thought about killing her but decided to let it go, for there would be others. He stood up, releasing her. Keeping up the front, she walked unhurriedly to the bathroom, where she busied herself, always watching him in the mirror, watching his glassy eyes. But he now felt that he had walked through this particular scene before, and was compelled to pay very little attention as he dressed, left the room and hit the street. Sunset, unctuous and alive, fertilized him again, sprayed a peculiar, twitchy laughter on him. He walked down the street; his dick got hard.

Watching through a dirty windowpane, Sera, though instinctively proud to have survived this wrinkle in the bed of a Holly-

wood motel, wished that she had someone to tell the story to...
no... that wasn't it. She wished that someone would listen to her
tell the story.)

She soon discovers that she's on a good streak, winning about
two out of every three hands. With her aggressive splits and
doubles she can win a few hundred dollars in no time, even
though her bets are relatively modest. She sticks around and
plays it through, mostly head to head with the dealer, as no one
else has gotten comfortable enough to remain in any of the other
seats. They remain mostly empty, occupied only temporarily by
the players who lack either the capital or sincerity to endure
prolonged play, who orbit the clusters of tables in any casino,
fidgeting endlessly with their ever diminishing silver and red
stacks of one and five dollar chips—never green or black, these
players—sitting abruptly at a table as though they were plunging
into a pool, and losing their nerve along with their money when
the half-life of their stack is reached; then rising, they fight their
way out of the tangle of too many chairs and back into the
periphery, roaming again the aisles or, tiring of that, the larger
scale territory of the gambling districts themselves. Sometimes
briefly the seats around her are semi-occupied by the desperate
tragedies who stand behind them with momentary resolve, putting at risk the last third, fourth, or fiftieth of the grocery money
or the rent, next week's paycheck or the remnants of a pawned
wedding band. They are not shaking or sweating, but they create
a tension thick with guilt and persecution. Their luck being
inversely proportionate to their need, they always lose. Sera is
disturbed when they appear, and turns away, not from the hope-
lessness of their situation, which they take far too seriously, but
from the intensity of their suffering, which will forever make
them victims in their own minds. Eventually her own luck turns,
her newly created little stockpile of green, twenty-five dollar

chips is now in jeopardy. She has already made and lost two bets on the dealer's behalf, so when she stands and he sneers, she simply thanks him and leaves.

At the cashier's cage she exchanges her chips for money and finds that she has won almost, but not quite, three hundred dollars; proving, she thinks grimly to herself, that tricking is still, for her at least, a more profitable gamble. She knows, though, that this money is different from that money. This money was once, and therefore will be again, chips. She and the casinos both know that chips are a wonderful, pretty tool, and possess none of the stigma of dollars. Dollars translate too easily into hours or houses or cars or sex or food or everything, and so losing a dollar is a much more tangible experience than parting with a chip, an object that looks more like a midway consolation token than a medium of exchange. To Sera, chips are the perfect symbol, symbolizing other symbols. It is this extra generation, the picture of a picture, that lets one become totally abstract about wealth in any degree; rendering it without meaning at first cursory glance, and inevitably, upon closer examination, with its most profound meaning; tying itself not to nothing, but to everything at once. She puts the cash, the once and future chips, into her wallet, interleaving it with her trick money as she arranges her bills. She is meticulous: all bills facing forward, right side up; new bills in back to be spent last, old in front—naturally; singles ahead of hundreds, and so on. She is so wrapped up in this familiar procedure that she bumps into a fellow cashee, who only glares at her as he places two small multicolored stacks of chips on the counter, one from each fist. He asks the cashier to count them separately. Sera hopes that when she loses money tonight it will be the money from the three boys, but now she'll never know for sure.

("Maybe you should get in. It will be best on you.")

The voice—some sort of accent—was emanating spectrally from the backseat of the car. She'd heard about this stuff and knew that sooner or later she'd have to deal with it.

It was all she could do to resist bending down and looking into the car, but she was afraid that if she did she would be lost. Instead she said, "Look, I didn't know, okay? I'll work somewhere else tomorrow."

A woman's whisper, then: "I'm not here to... Look at me! I'm not here to tell you where to work."

Sera felt the hands on the back of her shoulders, and then she knew that she would be in the car soon.)

"Time to take a walk, honey."

She feels an authoritative hand gripping the back of her arm. She tries to pull away but the grip tightens. Turning, she sees the long arm of a casino security guard.

"What's the problem? Let go of me," she says.

"We don't want you in here. That's the fucking problem," he says, "and you know it."

"I don't know what you're talking about. I don't know anything," she says. She tries painfully to free her arm with a fast downward jerk. "Don't worry. If you don't want me in here then I don't want to be in here. Just let go of my arm and I'll walk out."

"Yeah, we'll walk out right now, then we'll both be happy." He pushes her arm, forcing her forward very fast. His rigid march has her practically running to keep from falling. They reach the sidewalk and, without relaxing his grip on her arm, he grabs between her legs with his free hand and says in her ear, "Next time it won't be so fuckin' easy." He pushes her towards the street and turns back inside.

She is stunned. She looks around at the crowd of spectators. Baffled, their faces fixed in disapproval and apprehension, they look away from her and mumble nervously to each other. They move along. They have no time for people that get thrown out of places. They don't get thrown out of places. This scene, punctuated with that thought, makes everyone happy with themselves. They're glad that they don't get thrown out of places. They move along.

(A roller-coaster thundered overhead, then rattled down the track. The noise had frightened Sera, sending ice-cream down the front of her sundress; it quickly turned into a gooey, rainbow river, running down her chest, tummy and legs. Her father laughed and bent to clean her with his handkerchief. She looked about reflexively for her mother, a woman tormented by jealousy, and finding her nowhere in sight, embraced him.)

Sera looks for a cab. Momentarily forgetting about her facial bruises, she wishes she were dressed for work. She'd like to turn a good trick. She heads for the Strip anyway: better drinks, a more well-behaved class of security guard.

"Closed for remodeling. Try again," says the cab driver.

"No way. Since when?" she says, shutting the cab door and rolling down the window.

"Last week." He eyes her in the mirror. "You don't want to go there anyway. How 'bout the Sands?"

"How about the Trop," she says.

"All the way, the Trop. Mind if I play the radio?" He turns on the meter.

"Go ahead," she says.

Turning down his dispatch radio, the driver clicks on a small AM portable hanging on a chain from the rearview mirror. It spits static and fragmented music as he tunes in a station. "I don't usually do this, but you look like you wouldn't tell anyone," he explains.

"You're right, I wouldn't," she says.

"...Thank you, John, and God bless you," trebles the radio.

"We have time for one more caller. You're on the air. Hello? Reverend Phil? Can you hear me? Yes, you're on the air. Go ahead. Reverend, I just don't know what to think anymore. I mean, what exactly is happening in this city? You can't walk down the Strip without seeing those filthy newspapers, you know the ones with those naked girls all over them. The casinos are all showing those topless shows, those French shows. Everyone is drinking on the street. Reverend Phil, you talk about God but where is he? These people are all tourists. What's your name, dear. Jo. Well, Jo, sister—and isn't that a lovely name that Jesus gave to you, Jo— You know that Jesus is everywhere. We need to remember that the only way to fight the evil is to lose it from your mind, Jo. Look away from that devil. Look away from that pornographer. Look away from that robber. Look away from that murderer. The Lord will deal with them. Have faith, Jo, that they will be swept from this city. The drunk, the prostitute, the will not, live not suicides, will be swept away from our clean floor and into the pit to burn. Then you, Jo, and I and our sisters and brothers will walk again without the tainted presence of those that embrace the evil. Yes, Reverend, I know, but I don't understand. You don't understand, Jo. You don't have to. That's his glory. It's good or bad, us or them, black or white. Believe or burn, Jo. These books are written by the righteous. Do not dare to question that which can never need correction. This ark is long afloat, Jo. Come aboard and be safe. It takes no thinking. Pause not, and give only faith! Thank you, Jo, and God bless you…"

"What happened to your face?" asks the driver.

"My husband beats me," she lies, "but it's not really his fault. He just doesn't know any better. We love each other, so I stick around. Anyway, it's the only game in town."

"That's a shame, sister. You should lose that bum. Pretty girl like you could have any guy she wanted," he says.

She doesn't answer and they drive the rest of the way to the Tropicana easily, listening to easy-listening country-rock gospel songs.

Arriving there, she pays the driver and approaches the multi-tudinous glass doors which serve as an effective barrier against only the hot desert itself, and nothing else. Penetration of the first bank lands her in a half-ass air lock, in which she hears the muffled bells and buzzers from an army of gaming machines along with the faint remnants of the sound of traffic on the street, all led by the uneven thuw-wumping beat of the rotating revolving doors. Here the air has no temperature, or every temperature. So pausing only briefly to acclimate herself, she pushes onward through the second bank of doors and enters the casino proper, where it's always really loud.

She heads for the bar, choosing the side that gives her a spectators' view of the tables and machines. Waiting for the bartender, savoring the delicious complimentary goldfish-shaped crackers—so generously provided by this and many other atten-tive establishments throughout Las Vegas—she spots a well-appointed drunk at one of the blackjack tables who seems to be attracting some attention.

The fiftyish man is gaudily adorned with gold in every conser-vatively customary place on his person. He has that air of one who has and will spend too much of the evening teetering on the edge of consciousness but never quite passing out, and it is obvious that, in the morning, it will take the waxing collection of no-carbon-required markers, being generated even now by the floorman and initialed by both the dealer and the player, to help build a picture for his no longer self-sufficient memory. The nervous manner of the casino staff that is present indicates that this is a player with both the means and the inclination to lose a lot of money—a lot more money—tonight, here. The man is making barely intelligible bets of five hundred to two thousand dollars each on two simultaneously played hands, and losing almost all of them before he has even signed the markers for chips lost two bets ago. The floorman is desperately trying to keep straight his accounting procedure while patiently maintaining his most polite facade for the bleary-eyed player, whose sagging head seems on the verge of knocking over each new stack of chips. The man is far too drunk to remember his usual generous tip for the cocktail waitress, who does remember the last one and is feeling pity for him as he drops his empty glass into her hand and tells her he wants another J&B.

"J&B with a coffee back," she says hopefully, writing the order on a napkin on her tray as if she might forget it.

"Jayenbee with a Jayenbee back," he says to her, ignoring her.

Sera looks around for something better to watch; she doesn't want to watch this anymore. She once knew a man capable of such behavior. Almost self-destructive, it was in his case a way to prove his masculinity to—whom? Himself, is what Sera assumed, for all facets of his life were likewise overdone.

(He envisaged himself lusty and strong, vital and reckless, and indeed, in many superficial ways he was.

"I am an Arab pirate!" he confided in her, only moments before he ejaculated.

Sera, though touched by his attempt at openness, doubted the plausibility of such a notion.)

The bartender appears before her. "Yessssssss," he croons, dropping a napkin on the bar. He's a happy camper.

"Hi," she says. "I'd like a double shot of Herradura Silver tequila, please, and any bottled beer."

"Lime and salt?" he asks.

"Two double J&B rocks!" hollers the cocktail waitress from the service well.

"No thanks," says Sera.

"I didn't think so," he says. He gets the tequila and beer then goes over to tend to the waitress.

Sera downs all the liquor and half the beer almost immediately. She pushes her glass forward to indicate that she's ready for another. In lieu of working she has decided to drink a lot tonight. This is one of those rare times when everything seems to be getting to her. The normally undefined craving for companionship is making itself known to her and she doesn't like it. She feels strange, older. The incident with the security guard has disturbed her more than she can admit to herself. She cannot accept that she needs to be, at least at some deeply hidden level, or even in some insignificant way, accepted, validated like a parking ticket, punched.

Now the thoughts are raining, anxiety beginning to simmer. She wishes her fucking face wasn't bruised; there are at least four men at the bar who would pay to fuck her. One of them surely has a room here. It would be so easy. She thinks about what a great parking ticket she is, about the time spent before they come, when they are full of desire and, whether they know it or not, affection. She's okay with them then, okay enough to pay for, anyway. They squeeze their life into her, all they are, all they don't even know about themselves. Their biology stands at the helm of their bodies. That's a real fact, true on any level. Then and there, absolutely, though perhaps exclusively, she has value.

She feels the tequila in her blood, her veins. Her lungs fill with air, and again. The room is noisy, the seat hard. She is hungry, tired, sore, tipsy, self-sufficient, pretty, bruised, young, intelligent, unhappy, thirsty from salty goldfish, cognizant that that's the idea. She can get water. She has an apartment, a gynecologist, mail, cookies, and the means to bake or buy more. There is a government agency that makes sure that the cookies she buys will not harm her, and it works, she trusts in that. She is a part of her environment. She is still alive, an accomplishment that puts her in the ninety-ninth percentile, way, way ahead of most of her class. Her bruises, the security guard—these are the smallest of potatoes, an aberration. Nothing about this can put her down. There was never any question.

(Sabrina was a sixteen year old girl from Atlanta who had run away from home and, when they met, was making her way working as a maid in one of the small motels on the southernmost end of the Strip. The girl was, indeed, in many ways a sixteen year old, but in other respects she was atypically sensitive and kind. She gave a portion of her pay each week to a blind Mexican man who lived in an abandoned trailer, not far from the motel. This left her with food money and not much more. Rather than lose her or give her a raise, the motel owner let her suck him off after the rooms were cleaned in exchange for a night in an empty room, when there was one, as long as she cleaned it extra good in the morning and used her own detergent to wash the sheets. When the motel was full she would walk around the Strip all night, sometimes walking way down to Fremont, playing an occasional nickel slot or quarter keno. Sera met her sitting on the curb doing a crossword puzzle outside of a slot machine parlor one night. They talked until morning under the watchful eye of a giant, neon-clad clown. Sera found in Sabrina the first true friend of her life, and, deeming her sleeping arrangements less than desirable, offered the use of her apartment.

Three times they were lovers, each time without premeditation and most certainly without regret. Their mutual ability to do this was one of the strongest and most unique bonds that they had. They were both, by nature, very independent, and so had no trouble staying out of each other's way. They coexisted well for a while, but Sabrina was still very young and hadn't yet made any long term observations about herself, much less decisions. She grew restless and wanted to run away again but had nothing to run away from, a personal insult that she found impossible to come to terms with. Willingly she embraced heroin, losing her job early on, and taking up tricking in increasingly dangerous situations. She eventually disappeared, and Sera knew that she was probably dead in a Dumpster, or perhaps rotting in the desert after being chauffeured fifty miles out of town in the trunk of a Cadillac.

Sera was at a loss, dazed by the swiftness of decline; it was a syndrome that was very alien to her. It was outside the realm of what she was.)

Bells sound, unimaginably unnatural electric noises alert the patrons of the casino of the Tropicana that an event of temporarily great notoriety has taken place, is being publicized. The big winner is slightly annoyed at the distraction. She has other machines to tend to. The noise dies down. Sera watches Las Vegas's newest hundredaire pick up one of her hard won silver dollars—plenty more where that came from—and drop it back into the machine from which it came.

Laid off—*laid off*—growing ever more infatuated with her boycott of time and the devices that define it, Sera is allowing herself to slip in and out of an alcohol-assisted meditation and has no idea how long she has been sitting at the bar. The supply of goldfish crackers, apparently inexhaustible, serves as no indica-tor. The casino has made damn sure that there is no line of sight to the outside, so she won't know when it gets light. Eventually the cocktail waitresses will start requesting a disproportionate num-ber of bloody marys and screwdrivers. Vodka being a popular breakfast drink, this will reveal that morning has broken for the broke. The thought raises a point: it would probably be more convenient if it stayed dark for the next few days so she wouldn't have to plan on having her sunglasses with her; that is, it would be dark, and she wouldn't need her sunglasses. Bored, bored, bored.

(The Singers lived in the unit next to her first apartment in Las Vegas. She had been staying in a filthy little motor court on the grimy part of Las Vegas Boulevard South, between where it intersects with Fremont and where it is known as the Strip. She had finally, through careful, constructive deception and a large cash deposit, secured a real apartment off of Spring Mountain Road, not an easy trick for her, being new in town with no job. She had spent her last few dollars at K-mart on a clock-radio, a card table, and chairs, and was taking these into the new apartment when Mary Singer came dancing over to her carrying a glass full of flowers and another of white wine.

"Hello, Neighbor! I'm Mary," sang the woman. "Welcome, welcome! Put that stuff inside and we'll get toasted on rhino whino at my place. It's so good to have a new girlfriend! What's your name?"

"Sera." She couldn't help but be taken in by the enthusiasm, and she smiled warmly, extended her hand, and shook the flowers.

"Is that s-a-r-a or the other way?" asked Mary.

"It's the other other way, s-e-r-a. Is that m-e-r-r-y?"

They both laughed and were soon sitting on Mary's couch getting acquainted over German wine and potato salad. Sera explained, in response to Mary's query, that she was a cocktail waitress from Los Angeles, and that right now she's between jobs. Mary talked about her husband, Slim, and how Sera'll just love him and why doesn't she plan on dinner with them that night. This became the plan and they talked on, as newly acquainted women will:

"No, not yet," said Sera, "just a few boyfriends, but no one special right now."...

"Two years, but it seems like forever," said Mary. "He really is great. We met at the hotel. He had to fire me before he could

[ 35 ]

marry me. Isn't that a scream?"...

"I don't know. Maybe I'll go someday. I really don't mind waitressing. It's okay for now."...

"And that's it? Just towel dry in the morning? And it looks that good?"...

"Never. I can't, I'm allergic."...

"If I do you may have to put me to bed... Oh, why not."...

"Clinique, it's the best. I don't mind spending extra for that, I really don't wear it that often."...

"...was the worst! Slim's not perfect, but at least he pays attention to me. You know what I mean? I mean, I would say nowadays that I come almost every other time—well, one out of three—but anyway, that's tons better than my first husband. He would..."...

"Oh, no complaints. I really don't have the experience that you do."...

"If I'm interrupting you two I can go back to work," interjected Slim. Clad in tie and jacket, he stood grinning in the doorway. He looked hungry.

"Well, look who's here. Sera, this is Slim. Slim, Sera," said Mary, rising unsteadily from the couch, her half glass of wine riding along perilously.

They met and giggled and dinner went along nicely. Slim eyed Sera in a less than wholesome way on and off all through that evening and subsequent get-togethers, but she didn't mind so much; not only was she used to it, but the guy was just too bland to be at all threatening. She was happy to meet these people and let herself get caught up in being a neighbor. There were cookouts, shopping trips, expeditions to the Strip, nights spent barhopping, an uneventful and unique blind double date, set up by Slim with a pal from work. Slim made the predictable hints at physical interludes that he imagined would be shared by and kept between the three of them, and even showed up with champagne and cocaine at Sera's door one night as his wife bathed, presumably in ignorance. Sera skillfully let these embarrassing moments slide by without ever addressing the issue directly, and risk bruising his ego, but rather with a quick excuse and a flirtatious smile that would send Slim away not sure if he had been thwarted or flattered.

The Singers probably thought themselves closer to her than she did to them for two reasons: They were less guarded than she about being open, and they really never operated too far below the surface; so what was just friendly to Sera was often intimate to them. She was doing her best at maintaining a light friendship, and though she was indeed being deceptive about much of her life—a deception that caused her some distress—she had only affection for Mary and Slim, as, in varying degrees, she did for everyone.

Returning home one night after a very bad trick gone worse, bleeding and frightened, needing to be with another woman, she called Mary over. Mary was full of maternal concern as she sat listening in her bathrobe, clutching Sera's hands. She was quietly comforting to begin with, and gradually slipped into complete silence as the story unfolded. Mary's cup of tea grew cold as she sat for forty minutes, and heard Sera tell her the whole, relevant truth.

"Well don't worry, dear. I'm sure that Slim can find you something at the hotel, then you can put this whole nightmare behind you," said Mary, nervously rising. "You get some sleep and I'll call you in the morning."

"No, no, don't tell Slim. I'm fine. You don't understand. This was just a bad night. I shouldn't have bothered you. I probably exaggerated a little. Things aren't so bad," said Sera. She sensed that something was wrong but was in no condition to give it full attention.

But Mary was almost out the door. "Okay, our secret. You go to bed. Goodnight." She walked briskly across the lawn, entered her apartment and turned on the light in the bedroom, where Slim was sleeping.

The next morning Sera was awakened by her landlord, who told her to be out as soon as possible. "No later than the end of the month. And keep the place clean—you know what I mean—'cause I'll be showing it. I'm sorry, but this is just my policy. If you had told me the truth right off we could have avoided this whole thing. You can have your security back and I... well I haven't heard none of this," and he put an envelope in her hand and left the premises.)

She feels like shooting craps but is always put off by the rudeness of the crowd. These people are very intense about their game. They consider themselves to be the elite gambling force of the casino, the professionals. Their superior intellect and knowledge of the mathematics of probability are ever apparent in the pagan screams and howls that sometimes challenge even the slot machines' near monopoly on aural assaults. They make it well known that their complex work affords little time for toleration of one of the lower orders, say a quiet blackjack player looking for a change of pace. Should he be bold enough to penetrate the gauntlet of bodies, constantly squeezing shut any opening or flaw in its arrangement, he will be justifiably terrorized at the table. Arms will fall immediately into the path of his intended bets, his respiration will be impaired by giant plaided polyester warriors, spewing smoke, surrounding and almost engulfing him. Verbal abuse and humiliation will drive out the invader, a final sarcastic *excuse me* whipping his flank as he retreats back to his amateur world of childlike diversion, no longer an impediment to the progress of the real players.

Her ears absently fix on the tick-clicking of the casino's

money wheel, first accelerating rapidly and then taking forever to slowly come to a stop, each click lingering slightly longer in the ear than the previous one until the final surprising eternal *ick*, which merely precedes another in an endless series of spins. The dealer, banished to this isolated corner of the casino by a simple twist of shift rotation, paces his patter with the wheel. His pronunciation of options and possibilities is equally unenthusiastic for a big five dollar bet as it is during one of the frequent practice spins. The giant disk rolls redundantly, always and never moving, money riding its perimeter. Prisoners of the wheel, the decoupage dollars await the inevitable moment that they will spend frozen at the top, selected by a stiff piece of plastic. Bets on them, if any, will then be paid off.

On a perpendicular axis to that, the roulette wheel divides the world into red and black, even and odd, or the more specific numbered prejudices of one to thirty-six. Occasionally the freakish green zero or double zero, real losers, are favored by the silver ball. Blurred to the eye, rolling on a wheel, the little sphere rides its race indecisively, eventually dropping to the slower, lower track of imminent commitment. It drops into a slot for a while, then starts again.

At the blackjack tables dealers stand behind other dealers, awaiting their turns to shuffle up and take the house's chances against the inept infantry of American gamblers. The game can be difficult, for winning brings to a player careful scrutiny by the powers that be, and winning too much can cause him to be conspicuously ejected from the game and the casino. Bad players make foolish plays by definition; good players make foolish plays for the same reason, but only at appropriate moments. Fours and fives get split, so do threes and sixes. When? Why? The dealers watch quietly, knowingly. When they play in a player's seat they insure their blackjacks. See, they know this game.

Low key competence, pungent in the air of the poker room, always keeps Sera out, despite the informative flashes from the attendant. He is apt to make known to a passerby that a seat is available on table two, Texas hold-em. In this room players face players. The house doesn't care what happens here; it draws commission on all pots. Unlike the craps table, green is welcome here. Fresh players are chewed and digested in short order. The games continue with more cunning opponents. Methodically the money flows across the table from this one to that one, then to the new one, and back again to the first one, who is taking and giving, biding his time as he waits for one who isn't here yet.

The baccarat balcony is very quiet, well dressed and dignified. Many are the glances upon it from frequent players of other games who would never dare enter this realm. Beautiful women surrounded in black felt feign to play with each other. If a guy had a lot of money he could probably get fucked here. They never give up. It's all really neat, sort of European.

"More Herradura?" asks the bartender. He holds ready the bottle. He likes Sera, having identified her as an experienced but not habitually excessive drinker. He is, in his own domain, much like the better dealers who, spotting a competent gambler, will treat him or her as an insider who can be relied on to not do anything stupid or unpredictable, can be trusted to know what they want. More Herradura is served.

She is more than a little surprised at the ennui. It's not that she doesn't understand her life and all its implications, so far she does—as well or better than anyone does. But she didn't expect to be at such a loss simply because she can't work for a while. Her dependence on her routine, such as it is, has grown so slowly over the years that it has escaped her notice. Now that the coffee is on the wall, it's shocking for her to think that her life requires some sort of regular punctuation in order to make it manifest. Though maybe it doesn't, maybe it just does right now.

Like an experiment that is radically affected by the removal of one variable, her situation demands assessment. She can't really come up with one; in truth, she's not convinced it's that important. Drunk, she feels the odd inclination to take a long walk, right into the next few days; walking, then rolling, continuously. She leaves the bar and passes again through the hotel doors. Outside it's still dark and cool enough for this kind of walking. The relatively undiminished activity of pre-dawn Las Vegas raises her spirits, reminds her of why she thinks she originally came here. Long and straight, the sidewalk has inherited the desert's characteristic disregard for conventional distance. Here she can walk for hours, and since the Tropicana lies virtually at the end of the Strip, hours of walking are available to her.

She walks slowly, thoughtfully, observing as much as she can and allowing the alcohol to temporarily delay the waiting soreness. Walking now where she normally wouldn't, not looking for a trick where she normally would, she immerses herself in the perception of, without participation in, the business of Las Vegas. The hotels appear as mirages in the distance, and though each one seems to take forever to reach, they fall quickly behind her. Soon, where she has been looks like where she is going, so she apparently stands on the face of a mirror, the two directional options either identical or opposite to each other.

("Where? where are you going?" Sera whispered, so as not to wake him.

"Just away from him. I don't care, maybe San Diego," said the girl. Her purse fully stuffed with clothing, she wore baggy denim jeans with no underwear. She was the sort of girl who could make herself well-liked for one evening; that evening was a long time ago, and now only Sera would spend any time with her.

"Good plan. I hear tricking is a booming industry down

there." Sera regretted this sarcasm, and in fact had no heart for this conversation at all.

"Fuck you, Sera! You know you should be coming with me."

The marble was cold under her bare feet, so tucking her negligee between her thighs, Sera sat down. "I just don't think I could start all over again," she said.

The girl threw her purse over her shoulder. "Yes you could. You know you could, Sera. You of all people could." Then under her breath as she left: "You could do it a thousand times."

Rather than watch her leave, Sera went back to the bedroom and slipped quietly between the sheets, so as not to wake anyone.)

Stopping off here or there, she uses the rest room or has a drink of water. The montage of casino interiors lends more clearly a vision of their subtle differences. Not obvious things like decor or employee costumes, which are really just similarities, but the more significant indications of management and money. The type of gambler can vary widely from place to place, as well as the type of dealer. She never really thought of the casinos as having the same distinctions as other businesses, but now she sees that some make more money, keep things cleaner, have a happier staff than others. It just follows; there's nothing special, nothing universal.

("Will you talk to this girl!" Her mother stormed out of the kitchen, leaving her alone with her father.

"I know," Sera began after a long silence, after waiting respectfully for him to speak, knowing all along that she would speak first, that he wanted to listen to her, "that travel may not be a Darwinian imperative—"

"Oh, it is," her father corrected, then shut his mouth decidedly.

"Well then," she said, her suspicions now confirmed that her old ally hadn't failed her, "I guess we can also agree that certainly it must be, at least, broadening." And they both fell to laughter, though she could see the pain in his eyes.)

She's tired, has too much alcohol still in her blood. It'll leave her at its own glacial pace, regardless of how much she walks. She bears up, decides to execute directly the remaining two miles to her home. Her body wasn't ready for this. Some aches return; others take hold for the first time. As her head clears and the distance diminishes, she feels better. At home she lies down in her bed, sleeps until she wakes, is awake until she sleeps.

♣   ♣   ♣

"Who is there?"

"I have your cleaning, Mr. Fathi."

Gamal Fathi, a single gold chain around his neck, walks to the door of his hotel room clad only in a towel marked *Aladdin.* To him the hotel is a travesty which he finds repugnant, but it is also in a location that might prove useful should his Mercedes fail to start, something it has been threatening to do.

"Yes," he says, opening the door and taking the hanger and bundle from the boy. "This is it all?"

"Yes, sir," says the boy, though he was just asked a moment ago to make the delivery and has no idea whether or not it is complete.

Pushing a five dollar bill into the eager hand, Gamal Fathi shuts the door without a word of thanks. This gratuity, though it represents a substantial percentage of his capital, is woefully inadequate and embarrassing to him. He is accustomed to flashing much larger denominations; indeed, there was a time when he would not even trouble himself to pick up the change from a hundred dollar bill, preferring instead to handle only those decimally rich *see-notes*, the most visually appealing attempt in the monotone American currency.

Very much alone in the room, he drops his towel in preparation for a shower. In the corner of the room the bolted-down television plays silently, its screen absently graced by an oft rerun episode of Happy Days, but this is not the object of his attention. No, he is inspecting himself, standing naked in front of the mirror; he is inspecting himself and thinking of a woman whose nearness he can sense. Gamal Fathi would like to touch himself, but this is something that he cannot bring himself to do. And he intends to not have to.

"Inshallah," he says aloud to the mirror.

♣   ♣   ♣

*Klaaaaick......mmmmmMMMMMMMMMMMMMMMMMMMM,* the refrigerator turns itself on. It sounds happy, secure in the knowledge that it is doing its job; even if no one opens it, the food—or just the empty interior—will still be cold; you can be goddamn sure about that.

Sera rolls over on her couch. A sentence, she thinks, it's like a fucking sentence: mandatory vacation. The whole thing is irrational and new to her. Traditionally ignorant of the comfort of a real schedule, she's never before had to face the absence of one. For her it is far too restrictive, too involuntary to enjoy, and she feels no longer in synch with her think. Television amounts only to a series of cruel plays about people with purpose; she even envies characters who are killed on screen or doomed to die during a commercial. If faced with her own imminent death, she could at least release the relentless anxiety of futility. A suicide though, even one portrayed ineptly on a daytime drama, fills her with vexation, makes her feel alien to a species that can produce such options. Rejecting the contradiction, afraid of pursuing the logic, she has never pondered the line that runs between death

[ 44 ]

and death at one's own hands. It is a non-question, irrelevant. It is one of those tricks of reasoning that can only be seen on an abstract level, for brought to terms with bread and water, it comes undone.

♣   ♣   ♣

Barely a whisper, imperceptible movement of the dark lips: "I must still own her... she knows that I am here... she knows that I still own her and she is afraid to admit this to herself," but still the street, on this, his seventh pass, contains not the one he seeks. "I must have at least this one thing still in my life"—Gamal Fathi does not realize that he is speaking aloud, for these are not words that he would consciously pronounce—"this one thing, this one key to everything that I am, that she is."

The yellow Mercedes falls away from the Strip and moves in the direction of what he has learned is Sera's apartment. The clock in this car runs sporadically, on then off. The time it reflects seems always to have changed whenever he enters the car, though he has never seen the hands move. So it stands disadvantageously to even a stopped clock, which is assured of proudly facing the correct time at least twice a day. Gamal Fathi's determination unflagging, he has not admitted to himself his doubt, the impossible possibility that she has vanished from this city, and that this is the reason he has not seen her in—could it be two?—days. He must stay outside her apartment for longer this time, he resolves, must take a chance, must wait for some movement or a change of lights. She will emerge, he knows. She must work. Sera must work; this has always been her weakness, even at the start.

He has a plan. There is money left. There will be no mistakes, and Sera, as always, will do as she is told. After all this time she will suddenly see him: a surprise. He still has his eyes, the eyes that she could not share a city with, and they will burn their way back into her soul where they belong, where they have always belonged. One command—best if it is a trick on the street or at a bar—one task, one little fuck on his behalf, and she will be his, and he will be him. As it was.

But there is not all that much money, and the fuel tank is not all that full. Gamal Fathi, in his peripheral vision, thinks he sees the second hand of the dashboard clock move, but a direct look leaves this unconfirmed.

♣   ♣   ♣

Days—one? two? black plus blue—later, looking in the mirror, she is dismayed at what she expected to be an improvement in the condition of her face. The healing process, in its imperfection, is apparently working on an irregular curve. A new, unnatural spectrum seems to be developing under her skin. Slowly becoming discernible, it looks like it will get worse before it gets better. Her face has become a life-size, organic Polaroid photograph. Exposed then hand manipulated, it is trying out various hues before returning to its original, very perfect flesh tone. A new world of greens, blues and yellows covers the vast, swollen areas of her eye and cheek. She sort of purses her lips, then tries to frown at herself. This is definitely the worst number she's ever had done to her face.

("...but please, my friends, call me Al. It is my American name! I picked it myself!" The men at the table joined him in a hearty laugh, but without exception they were eyeing the pretty brunette who stood in the corner.

"Gamal... I mean Al, who's your friend? Is this the one you told me about?" Shrimp dip clinging to his moustache, and even to one of his diamond cuff links, this man secretly had his hand on his own erection as he nudged the man next to him, who failed to notice the contact through his own expansive middle. The other four men at the table—excluding Al, who stood—continued to stare at Sera.

"Ah, yes," said Al, his own eyes constantly darting to the fat buff-colored envelope on the table, "this is Sera. She is my gift to you, my new American friends from New York City. You may do with her as you wish in this beautiful penthouse suite, which is also my gift for the weekend to my new New York City friends. You will find her a very willing girl for all of you..." His skin a taut, healthy leather; his smile well-practiced and full, Gamal Fathi's eyes flared with meaning, and the natural magnet in him seized the table to a man as he said pointedly, "...just like we arranged."

Troubled, though too distracted by the coming evening to say why, the man with the misplaced shrimp dip looked up at Gamal. Now he smiled more because he felt he should than because he felt the smile. He said, "Of course, Al. I think you'll find this just as we discussed." He handed the envelope to the Arab.

"Where are you from, Al?" this from across the table, a well-built man, foolish and proud of the country he had been born into. "I mean, you sure don't talk like you're from this neck of the woods." A hint of contempt lingered in the comment, and the room tensed.

"No, you are right, my new friend."—Al was doing remarkable things with his smile—"How very observant you are." Then to the whole table as if in introduction: "I am from Oman."

"Tough place," said the well-built man.

Al smiled, now more broadly than ever, and said, "Yes, I hear this too. But I am not a tough man. I am a simple man who is here to learn from my new American friends." There was an awkward moment. Gamal Fathi made as if to embrace the entire table with his outstretched arms. "I must leave. The hotel service will bring you whatever you like. Enjoy these gifts." He turned and headed towards Sera and the door.

"I don't want this. Al, please, I really don't want this," whispered Sera, clutching his lapel as he passed.

"I want this, Sera. I need this!"

The voice was not that of a con man; it was real. It was the most real voice that Sera had ever known, and she once again, as with so many times in the past, pushed her needs into a little bubble, into a subset of the greater needs, the needs of Gamal Fathi. He was the man who had won her. He was the man whom she loved.

Al turned and addressed the six men. "Sera has asked me if she might undress at once for you gentlemen. She has a very beautiful undergarment which she would like you all to see."

The men all clamored as one in enthusiastic approval. Not one of the eight people in the suite doubted that Sera would now remove her clothing.)

Reflected in the corner of the mirror is her bedroom window. The translucent shade reveals that it's dark outside. Enough is enough, she thinks. She has done all the healing that she is prepared to do; any more time spent stagnant would do more harm than good. Opening her makeup drawer, she arms herself with an assortment of brushes, pencils, tubes, plastic boxes, mysterious disks, minuscule magic wands, wads of cotton, and so on. A skilled craftsman, she works for over an hour on what she knows all along is a futile attempt at making herself presentable. Outside of some brushed on, optically-illusory shadows, there is not much she can do to hide the swelling of her features. Also, since she is reluctant to overdo it to the point of looking ridiculous, the painting over of her discoloration has only a minimal effect. Her injuries are still too profound. She looks like a girl who got hit in the face and is trying to cover it up with makeup. She wraps up the effort as best she can.

But now the ball is rolling and she already feels better, almost elated. A cloud is lifting—visibly—each moment clearer than the last, each decision more perspicuous. Another glance in the mirror reveals that she is smiling, smiling to herself, as though considering herself newly recovered; as these things go, she can't remember ever before feeling so un-sick, or so anxious to again embrace her hard-won normalcy.

She selects from her closet one of what she likes to call her *fuck-me* dresses. Light blue, light weight, it is backless and slips easily over her head, calling for no bra. She rolls up her stockings and clips them to her garter belt, thus completing her synopsis of the potential architectonics of female undergarments. Already on, her panties are nothing more than two small triangles, black arrows pointing to each other: you are here.

Once again at the mirror, her eyes look at her eyes. She watches herself. Subtly transformed during the inspection, her face wears the partly impartial expression of assessment that is universally found in the gaze of any woman looking at her own reflection. She sees things here that no one else will ever see. Her scrutiny is infinite. Myriad computations, speculations, and judgments take place in this moment. Ultimately, with great magnanimity the face in the mirror is temporarily exonerated, until the next time it catches itself looking.

She finds her work purse and stocks it with lipstick and condoms, a few twenty dollar bills. With no intention of walking the Strip tonight, she has a cab take her to the Hilton. Set off the Strip and next to the Convention Center, it's usually pretty easy pickin's there. She'll be able to find a trick who's been in town before, attending conventions and tagging hookers. Some guy who's done enough to keep him from being too excitable, but not so impressed with his own savvy that he gets cocky. A local boy,

[ 49 ]

but not local here. She needs some straight, simple business. She tries not to worry about her face. These guys aren't that superficial. More smiles.

The main bar at the Hilton has a fair crowd. She can do this by rote. Seating herself in view of the room, making sure that there are empty chairs on both sides of her, she orders a margarita. This she drinks down halfway in short order, the balance to be slowly and conspicuously nursed. From the stage a cover of a Tony Orlando song blares out and fills the corner. She likes these gutsy, hard-working lounge singers and thinks that they take too much abuse. Of course she has to admit that anyone genuinely enjoying this music comes off looking foolish. At times it can sound good to her. She always wonders what the acts think of themselves; she can never tell. Across the bar is a young girl about to turn a trick. She avoids looking at Sera, though she is clearly aware of her presence. Talking to the girl is a lupine man with too much facial hair. He's very proud of it, wears it like jewelry. The men at the bar have scented Sera. The young girl resents the uninvited competition and shoots an icy glance at Sera, who smiles back at her compatriot. Sera has never understood why so many people choose contempt as the first option. She can't remember ever feeling that way.

"About ready for another drink?" asks an even looking conventioneer, materializing on her left.

"Yes, that would be great. Thank you," says Sera, still wearing a smile. "Are you here for the convention?" She has no idea what conventions are in town.

"Do I look that obvious?" he says. "My name's Paul." Extending his hand he shows exactly the same enthusiasm that he has offered to hundreds of business associates during the last few days. Sera guesses this and wonders if he would like to sleep with them, as well.

"No, of course not. Just a wild guess. I'm Sera, and that's a margarita." She takes his hand and nods at her glass.

The bartender is an older man who has spent most of his life at his profession. He has the drink ready almost before it is ordered. Likewise, Paul pays for it almost before it is served. A five dollar bill folded lengthwise and held between his two middle fingers has been moving metronomically, pointing alternately to Sera and the bartender. Paul is unaware that he habitually does this. It annoys his wife, who is at this moment giving herself a pedicure back in Pennsylvania, to no end.

"I couldn't help but notice," he starts, "that you have a few bruises on your face. What happened?"

"Car crash," she says. "Nothing serious."

"Oh…. Good." He seems to believe her. He's seen car crashes in Pennsylvania.

The girl across the bar gets up and, pausing to give Sera a nasty little smile, follows the wolfman out of view. That guy looks wrong. Sera hopes that she's careful.

"So," she tries, "are you alone, or are you just using me to make somebody jealous?"

"Alone. Alone. I'm here alone," he says quickly. "Can I buy you a drink?"

"You just did. Where are you staying?" she asks.

"Right here in the hotel. Why?"

Why. He said why. This catches her off guard. "Well, I thought that you might be looking for a date," she says, testing the water.

"A date! What, are you a hooker? What do you mean, a date? I just came over here to talk for a few minutes. A date? Have you seen your face lately? I've got a wife back home. And I'll tell you something else: The hookers in Pennsylvania don't run around trying to do—what do you girls call it? tricks?—tricks right after being in an accident!"

"I'm sorry," she says. "I guess I misunderstood. Please don't raise your voice. I won't bother you about it again."

"Sorry," he says, modulating. "Look, you seem like a nice girl and I was curious about your face. I'm just sick to death of everyone in this city trying to get my money. Have another drink. I gotta go." He leaves his change on the bar and walks away.

That, she thinks, is not exactly what I needed to happen here. She has a nasty feeling, an old feeling. It has been quite awhile since she's felt such a lack of control. Something is out of synch, and it is disrupting the ease with which she handily guides her nights.

(Safely on the bus to Las Vegas and thinking back for the first time, Sera was amazed at the timeliness of the elevator's arrival. Ten, five more seconds might have changed everything. She could still be there, maybe giving another sponge bath to that smelly accountant whom Al had sent her to the night before.

But it went her way. Things took over, or maybe things let go and she took over. Either way, when Al kicked her in the stomach, shouting *Leave!*, and turned back to his newest girl, Sera did just that. For the first time she really did leave, not just the room, but the apartment, and ultimately the city.

And he knew. He knew he had gone too far. He sensed a flaw in the glass. Waiting by the elevator, she heard him scream her name—a new and odd fright in the command. There was time to go back, and there was the distant whir of the elevator's ascent. There were these two intangible things with her in the hall, both playing out their purposes. Joining them, she held her ground; indoor-outdoor carpeting, and hard won, it was to be.

*Waiting* was something she was *doing*. Just like taking a shower or giving head, this was an executed action. Her part. She might have peed her pants—later they were damp—but she felt wonderful to have *done* this one thing.

Unraveling then, she saw the spool of her design, freely giving her slack as the elevator door opened and she stepped in, still not having heard Al's approach. The steel doors pressed themselves together to the faint sound of glass breaking. All the way down a voice in her head, or what she took to be the meaning of that expression, told her to continue *doing* things...

...and it will be okay, she told herself on the bus, now well past Barstow.)

"No deal?" says a hefty man who has rapidly moved into position beside her. He looks to be in his mid forties, excessively caucasian. His shirt collar is open and worn out over the lapel of his suit jacket, revealing an abundance of chest hair which continues up to his shoulders. Large and hard, his features are unified in a happy, arrogant smirk which smacks of malice.

She looks at him tentatively. "You've been listening in, Officer?" she says, though she knows he's not a cop.

"Officer my ass," he says. "Look, baby. You're not talking to some farm boy. I'm not that loser that just left. I know why you're here and I'm interested. What's the fare anyhow? Do I get a discount for looking at your punching bag face?" He laughs cruelly. "Just kidding. After all, it's not your face I want to use." He falls silent, as if to convey some special meaning, and looks deeply at her, as if there is anything he could possibly know. "Al sent me over—Arab guy—said you were a good sport. So how much?"

She must be very cold, for the hand on her back feels unnaturally hot. To her ears comes the fat man's voice: *Here he is now.*, punctuated by the annoying clink of glass from a passing busboy's cart. Now just a single finger draws an imaginary line along her spine, and as she turns to see who is behind her, she shivers.

Then she meets his eyes, and seven years vanish in an odious, bloodshot wink.

JOHN O'BRIEN

"Answer the man, Sera. He wants to spend some time with you," says Gamal Fathi. Up close now, he may be surprised at the condition of her face, but this has never mattered in the past, and his own remains as it is: very hard, quite pleased with the moment.

Sera looks away, out into the casino with its anthill of activity, a zillion people serving one common cause. Throughout her life she has never had, never even wanted to taste, a single moment of belonging to anything this big. She can't remember what hotel this is, though she finds that fact not disturbing in the least. She says, "Al," and she feels a longing for something that isn't here right now. She doesn't know what it could be.

The fat man moves his face close, right in front of hers. His cologne surrounds her, rudely attacking her eyes and nostrils. "C'mon, baby. What are you waiting for? I'm the man from Glad! How's five bills for an hour upstairs grab ya'?" he says.

"Okay," she says to him.

He turns and walks away, motioning for her to follow.

Al swiftly moves his hand to her wrist. "Give me the keys to your apartment, Sera. I'll wait for you there." He rummages through her purse, extracting her keys and some money. "Better hurry and finish your drink. You have a trick waiting that we can't afford to lose," he says. Then he is gone.

She feels sick as she tries to down her drink. Leaving it unfinished, she catches up to her trick at the elevator.

"What did happen to your face?" he asks. "If you don't mind telling me that is."

"Just some kids the other night," she says. "They got scared."

He nods, laughing.

They ride up to his room in silence. She feels apart now, strangely relieved, yet apprehensive. She is an observer again. He opens the door to the room.

[ 54 ]

"You girls always want to use the bathroom, right? So go ahead. There it is," he says. He goes on to the bed.

Sera closes the bathroom door and runs the water. She splashes her face, then urinates. Her hands are icy, her mouth dry. After catching a glimpse of herself in the mirror, she turns out the bathroom light and walks out in front of him. He's lying on the bed with his hands behind his head, looking very relaxed.

"Where's my money?" she says.

He gestures to the dresser. She picks up the money and tucks it in her purse, then undresses. She stands naked before him.

"What do you want?" she says.

He swings himself off the bed and removes his clothes. He is covered with hair and is more obese than she had realized. Hands now on his hips, he proudly displays a large erection to her.

"Lie down," he commands. "I'm on top."

She lies on the bed and spreads her legs. He mounts her. His quick insertion is shameless and painful. She winces as his wide hips spread too far her thighs, but she does not speak. He pounds at her recklessly, torturing her in a hundred different places, a thousand different ways. The wounds in her anus open, and she feels a warm trickle of blood blend with the sweat that is flowing into the sheets. She bites her tongue to keep from crying out, and he withdraws.

"You're holding up pretty well," he laughs. "Your friend Al wasn't kidding. How about some head."

She obediently starts to rise but he pushes her down.

"No, you stay there," he says.

He straddles her face and pushes his penis into her mouth, pinning her head into the pillow. Throwing his upper body against the headboard, he resumes the violent thrusting of his hips. She gags and chokes her way around attempts to participate. But he is only interested in fucking her face. His penis repeatedly hits the back of her throat. The intensity of his push snaps her neck back, and he grabs her hair to hold her head in place. Suddenly he pulls away and looks at her. He holds her head with one hand and, still above her, strokes himself with the other.

"I'm gonna come on your face, baby," he says. "I'm gonna come on your sweet black and blue punching bag bitch face."

His semen shoots onto her cheek. Dropping her head, he covers her face with his free hand and rubs his semen over her features and into her hair until, having extracted all that he can, his other hand slows to a stop. He rolls off of her and collapses onto the bed.

"Get lost," he says, giving her a kick in the side.

She gets into her clothes and only pauses for a moment in the bathroom, where she wipes off her face before leaving the room.

The wait for a down elevator seems endless, but finally one arrives.

(Tough trick, but at least it was a trick. Al found a trick for me.)

She goes into the casino and plays blackjack for about an hour.

(Everything is fine now; things are back on track.)

Betting modestly and only losing one hundred dollars, she shrugs off the loss and goes out to get a cab.

(There ought to be a stronger connection somewhere. There should be another level.)

She tells the driver where she wants to go and closes the cab door.

(Her father loved her in the super-sexual way that is far too sublime for incest)

The driver says excusememiss.

( )

The driver says excusememiss.

( ) ( ) ( )

"Excuse me, miss," says the driver, turning around, "but I can't seem to get my meter to run. It must be broken. If you want to, you can get another cab, or I can charge you a flat ten bucks for the ride. That's about what the fare would be anyway."

"Sounds fair," she says, first expressionless, then smiling too broadly at the potential pun.

As the cab pulls into traffic she looks in her purse for a ten and a five. She finds her compact first and opens it up for a quick look in the little mirror. She spots some dried semen in her hair. Damn, she thinks, looks like I'm going to have to stay up and wash my hair tonight.

"So what happened to your face?" says the driver, looking in the rearview mirror.

She looks up, a little surprised at the question.

"Nothing," she says.

## bars

## "BREAKING THE S

The bartender spins tri

bar with a wet, soiled

# OUND BARRIER!"

## mphantly and slaps the

## ag, but the sight of his

audience reminds him that he is already the acknowledged master of the morning lineup and must maintain decorum. "Breaking the sound barrier," he says quietly, authoritatively.

"Breaking the sound barrier?" guesses a contestant, three inches tall in an upper corner of the room. In saying it she changes the usual pronunciation of the phrase, placing the emphasis on the word *the* rather than the word sound. Those at the bar who are paying attention cock their heads and move their lips silently.

"BREAKING THE SOUND BARRIER," this the confirmation from the master of ceremonies, the host.

"You should go on that show." Any of several hoarse voices from the far end of the bar tend to assert this several times each morning.

The bartender nods in solemn assent.

Ben looks longingly at the television. It's ten o'clock and the game shows are at their daily peak. There's no longer any need to call in to work—he won't be in today, or tomorrow, or next Nsday—and the threatening-three first drinks of the morning, tall vodkas-cranberry, have been downed and kept down. He's ready to sit for a while and watch game show models display game show prizes, beautiful girls fuck expensive stuff.

His vision drifts past even the pseudo reality of the cathode-ray tube to a deeper level of fantasy. He is looking at a Hollywood grown American sweetheart, but he sees a dangerous looking woman clad in short leather and sheer lace. Black and disheveled, her hair hides part of her face. She gives the impression that she's probably just been fucked, or more accurately, that she's probably just fucked someone. Now she's looking at him, talking to him, ready for him.

*Just look at this fucking studio, Ben, she says, filled with glamourous merchandise, fabulous and exciting bonus prizes, including an extra special prize chosen just for you!: a big bad black BMW motorcycle, complete with saddle bags containing hundreds of thousands of dollars in United States Currency! So let's find a bar, get drunk, and go for a ride. Then we can get a suite somewhere, have room service send up a few cases of bourbon, vodka, anything you want, while we fuck ourselves silly. Then champagne for breakfast, and off on a wild fucking ride to some more bars. This is it, just for you, Ben, because you've been so patient, and because I want to fuck you, take care of you, and because there's nothing else in the world worth doing.*

Wait... whoa, yes: queasiness arrested. Perhaps a conversation is in order. No, not yeeeetttttt: stretching, shoulders back, a breath, a sigh. RoOoOoLlLlLiNg ThE nEcK, just like waking up. There, he thinks, that's better. He's ready to pick up his fourth drink. He's waited long enough, and now: *click*, his day can begin. The nausea has gone back into hiding; he must act, must be attentive to the timing. The fourth drink, and subsequent others taken at intervals of diminishing precision, will maintain his illusion of physical health. It will keep the sickness at bay for the rest of the day. He can stay well on his journey through hell. La la la la la la.

His eyes follow his hand as it reaches for the thin red straw. Failing to observe any shaking, any overt shaking, he plucks the straw from its intended purpose and drops it on the paper napkin under his glass. A small hemorrhage of cranberry juice forms a red blot on the cheek of a cartoon man with cartoon bubbles over his head: *My hife tusson mummerstan me.*

Ben doesn't need a straw now, at least not until tomorrow morning. He can pick up this glass as many times as he wants to, and never spill a drop. Click, click, click. He's back on track. Things aren't so bad. Feeling whimsically profound, he reflects on the parallel of his own ephemeral happiness—pursued, caught, sucked on—and that of the schoolteacher from Cleveland, who has just won thirty-two hundred dollars by solving the puzzle, *THE SKY'S THE LIMIT.* They both have their little prizes. They both started with their little clues. Hers was: a four word, fifteen letter phrase containing one apostrophe. His was: what you do every fucking morning.

Ben has his usual vista view seat on the lower end of the circular part of this particularly keyhole-shaped bar. Also present this morning are the bartender: always reading the *Los Angeles Times,* a small quantity of regulars: always reviewing the previous evening's drinking, and a well dressed—by comparison—business man who is downing the first of what will always be two glasses of tomato juice blended with beer. Alcohol leads to predictability. Ben knows none of these people. The only words he has ever spoken in this room are hi, vodka, cranberry, and thanks. In fact, what he likes most about this dirty little bar, one of several that he frequents, is that no one would ever look for or bother him here. He can be out and about, and still be alone with his liquor. But this is all painfully moot now; it has been a while since anyone has looked for or bothered him anywhere.

The television, perhaps the brightest entity in attendance, is certainly the brightest light in the room. This is a good thing; he does not want to see the source of the odor that rises from beneath the barstools. The place is very unclean, due mostly to the quality of the clientele, and though he resents the filth, he knows that it's an element in whatever draws him here. For his part he always makes it to the men's room sink before losing a drink. The sink is the preferred location for a quick puke, the toilet being far too nauseating for that purpose. Cranberry juice flowing red on white porcelain is money down the drain, but at least the next one is guaranteed to stay put.

Outlining the surface of the bar is a red vinyl cushion that is well perforated with rips and burns. It provides a soft place to rest his elbows as he cradles his chin in his hands and stares wide-eyed at the television. It outlines the bar in case he can't find it. It's a good outline for the bar, so he knows where it is. Outlining the surface of the bar is a red line for him to cross. Cross this line and you're out. He can cross the red line as he sits and stares at the television. He can cross the line and never leave the comfort of his own barstool.

This is his morning bar, his game show bar. But sometimes he happens to be here later in the day, during the hours that some lame sports spectacle is scribbled all over the television. He can't stand to stare at sports, so at those times he drops his gaze a few degrees and is rewarded by rows and rows of liquor bottles. Half real, they each stand in front of their own little reflection, doubling the fantasy. He examines the backs, the fronts, the sides. He monitors the volume of liquid remaining, the length of time that a particularly obscure bottle has been undisturbed, the accumulation of dust on its cap. He stares at red and blue fluids in the improbably shaped containers, until he begins to feel nauseated and quickly looks away. He wonders, given the caliber of the management, just how many of the bottles actually contain what their labels indicate, and how many are diluted or filled with cheaper brands, younger blends, knock-offs, generic vodka: give us a dollar and we'll make it work for you. He always has the same drink, his breakfast drink, but still it's like Christmas morning every time he walks in and sits down. Or it's like a candy store. It's like all the wonderful being-a-kid memories that he can recall, the good, the bad, and the easy. Make a wish, and your army of harlot bottles will respond. It is an unrestricted arena of choices; it makes what he gets, what he always gets, that much more attractive.

"We'll see you all again tomorrow. Bye Bye for now," says the TV host right before being drowned out by the applause of the studio audience, which seems to magically louden, as if by command. This is then replaced by a momentarily black screen and the reassuring voice of the network, "The fun's just begun and there's plenty more to come. So stay tuned all morning for plenty of laughs and prizes, starting with...."

That would make it ten-thirty, he thinks. He has one hour to kill until the real bars open. One hour until he can sit and drink pretty in the restaurant bars of West LA and Beverly Hills. That's when his day really begins. His stomach will be ready for bourbon and beer, or martinis, or whatever. He'll sit and drink away the afternoon, smiling and laughing with movie people, or west coast stockbrokers, exiled from their natural time zone, or anyone else who doesn't have to go back to work. One hour is just right. He'll go home, have a quick glass of vodka and a shower, put on some nice clothes, and be in Beverly Hills between eleven-thirty and twelve. Make it closer to twelve, say eleven-fifty. That way it won't seem like he's been waiting for the bars to open.

Time has become very important to him, much more important than it was when he had a job. Too many times he has awakened at three a.m., having passed out the previous evening, only to find nothing alcoholic in the house. He has felt the panic increase exponentially as the minutes click off the eternity between him and the legally wet world of six a.m.. His carefully laid stockpiles, meant to carry him over the tundra of two to six, were often consumed blindly from the abyss, after the line of careful laying had been crossed. Once he gave up and rushed to the all night convenience store, where he was grateful for the privilege of overpaying for a family size bottle of Listerine. Eight minutes later, parked in front of his apartment, the bottle was half empty and he had begun to calm down. He shut off the car, stopped the internal combustion.

So his life is punctuated by legislative break points and red flags of custom. At six a.m. the hardcore bars open and the stores can sell, though they sometimes choose to withhold, imposing their morality on some poor, sweating, shaking mess looking for his fix. Nine a.m. is considered a safe opening time for the bars that don't like to admit that people drink that early but can't let the business slip completely away; bartenders in these places tend to pause disapprovingly for an imperceptible moment before handing over a drink. The next milestone is eleven-thirty. At eleven-thirty everyone is willing to admit that the drinking day has begun and they proudly open their doors and pour their drinks. It's smooth sailing until midnight, when, if they haven't already, the more reputable bars bail out. Any place that stays open passed midnight is probably good until two—actually one-forty-five—the most important time of all. Never let two o'clock happen unless there is more liquor in the house than you could possibly drink in four hours—no small quantity.

It takes about five hours to drive from Los Angeles to Nevada, land of anytime alcohol, and there are no commercial flights at that hour. Teasing, gnawing, when you're out of liquor at two-thirty in the morning it looms, conceptually bad, in the back of your head. Ben has often thought it through, but it's just not a solution; by the time he would get there the bars would be open in LA.

It's ten-thirty-one. Ben drains his glass and stands up. He mutters, "thank you," and turns toward the door without waiting for an acknowledgement. Outside it's still overcast—spring in Los Angeles. He walks straight and sure to his car. He feels okay, swinging up.

On his way home, having stopped off at a liquor store for a can of beer to drive by, Ben feels elated. His day is in gear and he has everything to look forward to; he has a plan. Things will tick along fine now. He turns up the radio and thinks about what album to listen to while he gets dressed. Checking his pocket, though he already knows its contents, he confirms that he'll need to stop at the automated teller machine.

Money, money. He's going through a ton of money these days. When he lost his job last week he gained a sizable final check; his former employer really liked him and felt terribly guilty about having to fire him. Never mind that he unwittingly delayed the dismissal meeting by staying all morning at the bar and, after checking in with the receptionist, was on his way out for an early lunch when his boss caught up with him. Ironically, had he known what was in store for him that morning, he would have made it a point to be on time; he is very conscientious in that way. So they called him in—by then he did know what for—and asked him to leave. He felt so bad, not that he was being fired, but because his boss was on the verge of tears. How could he blame them? For the last year and a half his daily routine had been: Come in late, say eleven; flirt with the receptionist; go to lunch early, eleven-thirty; return from lunch late, about three; copy must-do list from today's calendar page to tomorrow's; walk fast around the office; leave early, no later that four-thirty. Everyone knew it for almost as long as he did, and he knew that they knew. It all just flowed so nicely that no one wanted to fuck with it. Not that he didn't have his value, he did. He could be counted on to, at least, not let anything become a crisis, and he fixed everything that broke. The latter was not even required of him, but he could, so he did. He knew that being *handy* is the kind of conspicuous skill that makes it easier for others to tolerate you. They tolerated, and even liked him, for as long as they could. They eased their guilt by cutting him a padded check. Chockful of make believe vacation pay and sick leave, and iced with severance play pay, it was intended to help him get back on his feet while he looked for another job. But they knew and he knew that what it really represented was a whole fucking lot of booze.

Money, money. His final paycheck, added to what was left of his once substantial savings, gives him a net worth of around five thousand dollars. On top of that, he can wring at least that much again out of his credit cards; he's always been a good boy, and it will be sixty to ninety days before little flags start appearing next to his name on monitors and printouts from here to Arizona.

Money, money. That gives him ten thousand dollars in drinking money. If he stops paying his bills, and only pays, say, one month's rent, and keeps up his virtually non-existent social life and eating habits, then it can pretty much all stay drinking money. If he drinks one hundred dollars a day—and he can—he's got one hundred days to drink. It's just an arithmetic operation, simple logic.

In his kitchen he picks up the bottle of vodka. Center stage on the white tile counter and always threatening depletion, this is his home bottle. This is his sick bottle, his too-late bottle, his one for the road bottle. This is his utility bottle; it keeps him at his default setting. He pours a tall glass and cuts it with a splash of tonic. It's quite a lot of vodka, and it represents his last hurdle of the morning. He feels all right now, but if he can get this down he knows that he won't embarrass himself in public. Throwing up at your barstool is frowned upon in Beverly Hills. He carries the full glass into the shower with him, just to be on the safe side.

All goes well, and by the end of the shower he's feeling great. Craving music now, he drips over to the stereo without waiting to dry and plays one of the twenty-some cuts that he tends to play over and over again when he's been drinking, that he tends to play over and over again. He pours another drink and dances back into the bathroom for an ambitious morning shave.

To Ben, shaving is evidence that everything's fine. These few minutes of socially suggested practicality tend to convince him that he, like the rest of the normal world, is just living his life. He's just another guy that gets up and goes through a regular routine, wades through a non-spectacular day, and comes home and goes to sleep. He's a cog in the machine. He's a soma-driven epsilon who happens to be plagued with imagination. For instance, his habit is to shave around his mouth first; that way, he can sip his drink even if he's not finished shaving—his mind never rests.

He looks in the mirror and doesn't care that he is an alcoholic. The issue is entirely irrelevant to him. He does all this deliberately, with purpose. Yes, of course I'm an *alc*, he thinks. What about it? It's not what the story is about. There are a million ways to croak; he's only plucking a piece of life. Let go and fuck God. There are a thousand mind manipulations. As he and his friend used to joke about: It's time to cut your hair, get a job, and just give up. Ha Ha. The crime is not that he's an alcoholic; big deal! The crime is that he's disoriented, big time.

He gets dressed to the music, sometimes dancing with himself in the mirror: will you go out with me? He puts on too much too expensive cologne so he can stink of a different kind of alcohol. Tie done up right and suit looking sharp, he spins on his heel and walks into the living room, where he trips over the low coffee table and crashes through its glass top. He groans once and then starts snoring.

♣   ♣   ♣

Very still now in the apartment, much like it must be in any empty apartment or house, families at work, perhaps on vacation. Ben is in communion with the rest of the motionless stuff that patiently occupies space and waits to be fucked with; he is an object of his own device. The refrigerator clicks on and off, faithfully cooling its near-empty interior, pursuant to its agreement as a major appliance. A hand moves on a clock—actually, all the hands move on all the clocks—but to all intents and purposes, it is silent. A heart is beating. Organs are deteriorating. There is something forbidding about this place. It can be felt between the thumb and the index finger, like noxious paint fumes to a blind man. The sighted might observe that the paint is a very bad color indeed and either leave now or pine for the previous coat.

When Ben awakens it is dark. Panicked, he instinctively looks at his watch. It's ten-thirty and he relaxes a little. Disturbed glass clinks and crunches as he gets to his feet and shakes himself. This day is shot, but everything else seems to be in operating order. By way of a test he walks to the kitchen: slight soreness, no blood so far. What a fucking mess. He drains the vodka bottle into his glass and goes to the mirror, no blood at all. After brushing the broken glass out of his hair and replacing his ripped suit coat with a sports jacket, he walks down the block to the liquor store and buys a couple of fifths, so he can deal with this unfortunate twist in his day and come up with a plan for tonight. Actually, he feels pretty well rested.

He can make the walk to the liquor store okay now, other times just barely. He misses walking, the brisk hikes down the boardwalk in Venice, or along the canals, or not so brisk walks on the sand, where the outcome of each step is too unfamiliar to master. Walking made him feel independent, a fast moving visitor observing the lives of those whom he passed. He used to walk fast, faster than anyone else, though it was never an effort for him. He would just cruise along comfortably at his normal speed, passing everyone on the sidewalk and causing any unfortunate companion to alternately walk fast and jog in order to keep few their trailing paces. He used to walk everywhere—the library, the grocery store, the mall in Santa Monica—now he drives. Physically crippled with alcoholism and psychologically afraid of being too far from its source, his walking radius has become the distance from his front door to his car. The liquor store falls just a half block outside of this parameter, so he makes an exception. But he does miss those long fast walks. That was something he could do better than anyone he's ever known, or known about.

On his way home from the liquor store he falls behind a beautiful girl walking her dog. He hasn't seen her face, but she is beautiful from behind. Not just her shape, which is quite nice, but her whole walk, her feeling and movement. This girl is pleased with herself. He considers for a moment that this may be the only art that he remembers how to appreciate, and he's not sure if that's a good, bad, or neutral aspect of his personality. She is beautiful right now. If he never sees her face, or if he sees her face and doesn't like it, she is still beautiful. He views this particular opinion as a refined and matured version of how he would have felt as a boy; back then he would have hoped that she had a pretty face. He still does, of course, but her beauty is, for him, no longer dependent on her face. He thinks about her panties as his mind wanders, encompassing her in an overstated fantasy. Panties may be a bit too specific for a short walk behind an unknown girl. Again he wonders if the mental twist is positive or negative. Positive, he decides, you can never be too specific. But then, the infinitesimal must be, by definition, as infinite as the infinite. She has stopped. All of a sudden he is beside her, looking into her inquisitive face. Disappointed, he smiles and walks on. She is very young indeed.

Back at home he has a couple of glasses of vodka, washes up, gets dressed again, and refills his glass on his way out the door. He's decided to drive to Beverly Hills and catch last call at one or two places before wrapping up his night at some of the grittier bars which are closer to home. His driving, as usual, is pretty even. Weaving is for amateur drunks, not for him. More than once he has driven alongside a black and white for miles, totally stoned and unconcerned. He knows that he won't fuck up by driving sloppily and getting busted; he'll just fail to react quickly to a situation one day and either kill himself or someone else. He finds this latter possibility, murder, intolerable, so he tries not to think about it.

Last year he got stopped on the 405, the San Diego Freeway. It was four a.m. and the road was almost empty, so he was going ninety-five down the hill. That type of overt violation was unusual for him, but he had snorted a lot of cocaine that night—even more unusual. He didn't like drugs and was anxious to get home to his nth drink to help cut the coke; he really didn't like drugs. He happened to look out the open window to his left, only to find a CHP motorcycle cop pacing him—no lights, just pacing him. The cop waved and he waved and smiled. The cop indicated with his hand that Ben should pull over, so he did. Ben got out of the car and stood by the driver's door waiting for the cuffs.

"Going pretty fast," said the helmet clad cop.

"Yeah, I guess so. I'm pretty late getting home. Is there any lipstick on my face?" said Ben, stretching out his neck for inspection, and surprised that he had said this before thinking it over.

"Where's home?" asked the cop.

"Venice," said Ben. Without being asked he extracted his license from his wallet and handed it to the cop, who ignored it.

"Slow down," said the cop as he mounted his motorcycle. "Go home. It's okay."

So Ben got in his car and pulled away. Driving home carefully, he turned the thing over again and again in his mind. He didn't feel the slightest bit cocky or smart, just intrigued. He never understood that little piece of good fortune.

Apart from speeding on the 405, the only other really silly thing that he did while driving drunk was to break his own car window. He had just finished a bottle of beer and dropped it on the car floor. This was a habit he had, preferring to dump his empties in a trash can rather than litter the streets with them. This little bit of environmental consideration worked fine, but on a few occasions the likelihood of an official presence—say, a toll booth, or an impending U-turn—compelled him to purge the vehicle of what might become evidence, that is, empty beer bottles. This happened in Laurel Canyon one night. Not going especially fast, he nevertheless thought he saw a cop pull out of a speed trap behind him. Just then the thickly foliaged road went around a sharp bend, so to be on the safe side, he picked the empty beer bottle up off of the floor and chucked it out what he thought was the open passenger window. Next came a tremendous *pop*, as safety glass showered the car's interior. The cop turned out to be a false alarm and Ben couldn't stop laughing about the window, which he purposefully never had replaced. The next day he even found the bottle, unbroken on the back seat.

As he crosses into Beverly Hills he is extra cautious, wary of that city's super-saturated police coverage. He parks on Crescent Drive, in a semi-residential section, far enough from the bars to not be seen walking directly from car to bar and back to car, one of many extra precautions that must be taken when drinking hard in Beverly Hills.

The lights are already up at what was to be his first stop, and though they know him well there and would serve him after last call, he passes by. He needs to use his plastic whenever possible now and save his cash for the days ahead. Beverly Hills is much better suited to alcoholism on credit than Venice is. But to go into a place that does the courtesy of serving you after last call, only to have you pay with a credit card, well that's just bad etiquette. There are other options, it's only midnight.

Miles from, but heading towards the water, he strolls down Dayton Way. The *way* streets run perpendicular to the *drive* streets, but that's about where the right angles end. If Wilshire is considered as the $x$-axis, then there aren't too many verticals and horizontals to be found in Beverly Hills. If Santa Monica is $x$, then you don't know your north from your south. The streets are nice, but not that nice. This city has an exaggerated reputation. There's plenty of money here, but that's true of a lot of places. The daytime population couldn't be anymore average, at least not in southern California, and at night the restaurants are filled with tourists and valley people, rechecking their check totals and calculating tips. Beverly Hills is just a nice part of LA, without the meaning, even though it isn't really part of Los Angeles at all.

He slips into a place that stays open a little later. The bar is half full, and most of the patrons look as though they've been there awhile. He likes bars at this hour. People who are still drinking at midnight tend to like drinking, enough, if not as much as he. It's the next best thing to a bar at six a.m.. That's the best, no pretense. People drinking at six a.m. are people drinking all the time. It's out on the table: *Good morning... Mornin'... Good morning... Hi... What can I get you?... How are you this morning?... Scotch and milk... Good Morning... I'll have a whiskey and water, please... Say, have you ever tried seven and seven?... Oh please! I can't take all that sugar first thing in the morning... Good morning.* Ben orders and receives a double shot of one hundred and one proof Wild Turkey and a bottle of German beer. He sits and drinks, orders more and hands over his American Express card as collateral. He sees a girl sitting alone at the bar. Actually, he was aware of her the moment he walked in. Now he looks at her. She smiles and looks back at her drink. He walks over to her.

"Good Evening," he says.

She pulls away and wrinkles her nose. "Been drinking all day?" she says.

"But of course. I'm Benjamin—Ben," he says. He hates that. For the life of him he can't understand how everyone can smell him a mile away. It's very frustrating. No matter how much he bathes or gargles or perfumes, he still smells like booze. It must be such an integral part of him now that it has become his natural odor. That would explain why he can never smell it, neither on himself nor on anybody else, not even other drunks.

"I'm Teri," she says. Ben extends his hand, and pretending not to notice it, she cups her glass with both hands and drains it through the straw. She lets it gurgle for an extra beat to make sure that he gets the point.

"I'll get you another one," he says, downing his own double bourbon, "and me too. Mind if I join you?"

She forces a smile, but she also wears the expression of a dog getting a bath with a cold hose. Seeing that he is very drunk, she is disappointed. When he walked into the bar she had imagined a different situation.

"Why don't we have our drinks and go to my apartment at the beach. We can watch a movie and I'll mix you up a gooey blender drink," he says. Inside he winces. Part of him realizes how stupid this is. It's his little defense mechanism that kicks in and trashes his credibility whenever someone is threatening to show an interest in him. It dawns on him that he has crossed over the line that runs between maintaining alcoholic and sloppy, stupid, obnoxious drunk. But at least he is cognizant of it this time; he'll try to ease off.

"Oh, thank you, but I don't think so. I'll just finish my drink and go. I have to get up pretty early tomorrow," she says.

They get their drinks and both take long swallows. By now Ben is obscured from himself. He can no longer monitor his actions. He can't edit himself. Later he will know, but right now he doesn't, that this is not him.

"I really wish that you'd come home with me," he says, slurring and breaking his words. "Yourso cute, and I'm really good in bed... believe me... yousmell good too." He stops and frowns. "No, okay," he mutters into his glass. He swivels on his stool and his arms find the bar for support.

She starts to speak and then doesn't. Looking at him, she gets a look of great sadness in her eyes, sadness so intense that it goes beyond what her face has made you believe she could feel. Ben does not see it, but it is not wasted. It serves more purpose to her than it possibly could to him right now; she did not consciously author it, and she is surprised.

"Maybe you shouldn't drink so much," she says. "I have to go. Thanks for the drink." She gets up and walks quickly to the door.

Her understatement seems to give him a spark. "Maybe I shouldn't breathe so much, Teri!" he calls after her. "Ha! ha!" But she is gone. The bartender shakes his head and puts down the glass that he is washing.

"Time to go, bud," he says. "We're closing up."

He puts Ben's credit card on the bar and waits for the signature. Ben fills out the tip and total and signs the slip, then removes his receipt and adds it to the growing collection in his wallet. He must remember to throw those things out.

The always depressing experience of leaving a bar creates a sense of loss in him that gives his mind a little jolt. He should immediately proceed with the evening; it is getting late. His watch is accelerating as it nears two, and why not? he thinks. It always takes a long rest from two to six. There is time for only one stop at a bar near his home, but first he will stock up at the store. He has just enough cash left. The trip to the ATM, cleaning up the broken glass at home, that sort of stuff can wait for the wee hours, when he has nothing better to do.

Walking to his car he feels odd. Things could start crumbling fast now. He stands on the ledge, about to lose control of his handle on the world: alcohol. He's ready for this, ready to sit back and watch. Time is now the biggest irritation in his life. Las Vegas looms in the back of his head. Free from closing hours, lots of liquor always everywhere, it is inevitable that he will end up there. All he has to do is remember not to gamble drunk, which means not to gamble at all, and he can make his money last long enough to comfortably wrap things up and have fun doing it. Part of him is afraid to go, aware that this crystal-clear thinking is bound to elude him in Never Enough City. In any case he must go to the bank soon, during real hours, and withdraw most of his cash, leaving a token amount that he can pull out anytime from an ATM in Vegas, or wherever. He should have all his cash at hand; who knows what could happen? The bottom line is, now more than ever, always have access to a drink. Always have access to a drink.

At the store he can't bring himself to buy a half-gallon of cheap generic vodka. Remembering that there is still some at home, he settles for a fifth of Polish Vodka instead. Why fuck up at this late date? Purity of execution will only add to the artistic aspects of the whole wretched mess. So with the finality of this resolution keeping his chin up, he waits impatiently in the twelve items or less line. It's okay, he thinks, I have less than twelve items.

To him a daily benchmark is his final seat at the last bar of the night. It is his regular stop near his home. He doesn't like the place much and wouldn't normally go there, but the location is too good, too convenient. Suited well to the public safety, this place oozes its smoke laden atmosphere of tough fuck biker talk and dirty women out onto a sidewalk that travels less than two blocks to Ben's front door. This allows him to drink lethal quantities with no worry of dropping off at the wheel, for there have been occasions when even he knew that he couldn't possibly operate a motor vehicle with any degree of intelligence, much less safety. So if he should wake in the morning and find himself with neither his automobile nor the recollection of where it might be, he has only to stumble down the street and around a corner, and there it will stand, secure where he must have left it the previous evening, more or less in a parking space.

He sits at the filthy bar, amidst the leather vested fat guys, the worn and weary pool tables, the smelly sluts who are much harder and drunker than he'll ever be, the puke-piss-spit-blood en-crusted carpeting, the brain-damaged human carcasses who have held their heads below their shoulders for longer than he's been alive, the slimy sidewalk penny-loafers who wanna be his pal, and the rest of the supporting cast with heads vacuous and pant seats full. He sits with his glasses and bottles in front of him. He sits as the last remnants of today and all that came before it slip into the void of blackout. He sits at the filthy bar and silently witnesses the change of watch from his will to his independently operating motor skills. His heart provides the musical accompaniment as the drinks are finished and he walks his crooked line home, as he clutches his bag of vodka and makes the distance to his door, as he puts his parcel on the floor carefully—even his body knows how important it is—and stumbles to his bed, where he turns off. His heart is beating him to sleep; there is no more required of him for now.

♣   ♣   ♣

It is a different day, and Ben sits in a different bar. It is early afternoon and he has successfully made the trip into Beverly Hills for lunch: a bullshot and six raw oysters, continuous vodka for dessert. Now properly fortified, he is ready for a second visit to his bank, also in Beverly Hills.

He tried earlier, and it didn't go so well. He giggles over his kamikaze, under his breath, "My visit to the bank didn't go so well this morning." He had felt okay after his morning drinks and decided to take advantage of his consciousness and withdraw the rest of his cash from the bank. This sort of big business deal is not his favorite thing to do these days, and the bank is ripe for construction as enemy turf by his often paranoid, alcohol-en-

riched imagination. In an attempt to get the nastiness over with—
actually just the simple process of cashing a check since he did not
intend to close the account—he decided to stop at the bank before
starting his afternoon drinking in Beverly Hills. He had filled out
and signed the check beforehand, four thousand and six hundred
dollars—4.6K, his life expectancy—but forgotten that he would
be asked to sign the back of the check in the teller's presence.
Upon hearing the words *Would you sign the back for me please,
sir*, the small tremor in his wrist immediately doubled its seismic
output. Just being partially sober in a bank was already enough to
produce serious sweating, but to have to sign a check under the
gaze of a teller was unthinkable.

"You couldn't just cash it like that?" he asked with his best
flirtatious smile and sweat lining his neck.

"I'm sorry sir. Is there a problem?" said the teller.

Fuck, fuck, fuck, nowhere else to go.

"Well," he started, his voice cracking, "to tell you the truth,
I'm a little shaky right now." Just a little, he thought. "I had a
rough night and I guess I need a little hair-of-the-dog." Hair-of-
the-pack, he wanted to say. "Why don't I just come back after
lunch when I'm feeling better. We can take care of it then." He
picked up his check, in itself an accomplishment, and left.

The poor girl smiled through her confusion, wondering if
even this customer could possibly be right. Certainly he was not
all right. How could she know that there was disarray and
devilment wreaking havoc with his very biology. To her he was a
customer of the bank whom she recognized, but who refused to
sign his own check. She thought it over, and since her cash drawer
had not been opened at all during the encounter, she shrugged it
off.

While listening to the lunch waitresses shout their orders to
the overworked bartender, he spots his moment. Time for the

bank. The bank once and for all, last and forever, is about to be revisited. He gulps the balance of his drink and calls to the bartender that he'll be back in a few minutes. He has never walked on a tab and this is standard operating procedure for him. He and his ego say smugly to each other, *They know me here.*

He is cruising on that golden highway of maintenance. The increasingly elusive mixture of blood and alcohol that makes him feel and act normally happy. This is the time of his grand hallucination. Things are fine. Who knows what could happen tomorrow? He's getting away with a lot of fun. What it really is, is a taste of his first good drunk. It's a small refresher course in the wonders of alcohol. Start again at zero, add one, and go! You have x minutes of fuel remaining. Enjoy your flight, and stop by our Abyss Cafe for a bite when you get sick of Club Average. It's the last turn before the terminal.

"I'm back. I've got my check. I'm ready to sign, baby," he says with a wink to the same unfortunate teller. He flips the check over and signs it with an elaborate gesture. "Steady as a fucking rock. Wanna have dinner with me?"

She counts out his cash and glares at him as she hands it over. "I'm glad to see you're feeling better, sir," she says coldly. "Do you need a validation?"

That sounds pretty good to him, but even if she meant it, she wouldn't know where to begin. At this point he's not so sure that he would either. He puts his money in his pocket, thanks her and leaves.

He goes back to the bar to fortify. The abundance of cash in his pocket is flirting with him, and he knows that he will have to blow at least some of it, despite his painful awareness of how crucial it is to his future that he be sensible and save it for drinking. He's not sure if, given the circumstances, this particular future would be considered long term or short term, but regardless of its categorization, it, like all other futures, must be attended to. He peels two hundreds away from his fortune and puts them in his pocket with his other petty cash. The remaining forty-four are shoehorned into his wallet which kinks and bulges in protest, never having expected to bear such a burden.

The habit of keeping cash in his left front pocket grew out of an emergency that occurred some months back. He had awakened well into withdrawals and was very shaky. Having nothing in the house he hurried to the liquor store only to find it inexplicably closed. With his shaking accelerating he was already unable to drive anywhere, so he made for the bar down the street from his apartment. By the time he reached it and ordered, his hands were in such turmoil that he could not extract a bill from his wallet. The disapproving bartender, an older man who thought that Ben was too young to be in this condition, eventually agreed to go into the wallet and get the money. Four drinks and forty minutes later Ben was recovering, but the whole incident had been so embarrassing, not to mention too very close for comfort, that since that morning he has always kept at least twenty dollars in his front pocket. In this way, no matter what his condition, he can always manage to shove his left hand into his pocket, clutch the money, and drop it on the bar or counter. The whole setup made so much sense that he got in the habit of keeping all his cash there. Not only does it prevent a pickpocket from separating a drunk and his money, but it keeps him that much closer to his liquor, a circumstance that is always the subject of his best interest.

Swirling down the hoary bourbon and feeling good enough to hold it in his mouth for a moment and appreciate the taste, to savor the bouquet as it rises and fills his throat and sinuses after he swallows, to know the hearty burn as it hits the stomach and begins with a punch its assault on the body, his mind drifts to the little bank teller. Perhaps not remarkable physically, she is the most recent female contact of record, and is certainly... serviceable. But is she desirable? Is she irresistible? Maybe if she drank bourbon with him it would help his opinion of her. Maybe if she drank bourbon and then kissed him, and he could taste the sting, maybe that would help. He might like her more if she drank bourbon with him while they were naked. If she smelled like bourbon and fucked him, that would increase his esteem for her. He could probably learn to love her if she poured bourbon on her naked body and said, "Lick this, clean it up." He would really dig her if she had bourbon dripping from her breasts and vagina, if she spread her legs and poured it on herself and said, "Lick this, drink here. I'm a mess." Or what if she got fucked by a lot of guys, big guys who liked fucking her, and they all stank of bourbon and come and she said to him, "There! See! I have a purpose. I have a place, and a value. These guys like to fuck me and now I stink of their come. That proves that I am worth something, and the closest you'll ever get to being worth anything is to clean me up. Put your stupid fucking face on me and lick up that come and booze. Lick me clean so I can go fuck someone else. That's what you get. You can aspire to be Apprentice Sloppy-Cunt-Licker. How's that sound? Your fucking validation in your face!" How very strange that would feel, to be so well understood.

He finishes his bourbon and talks the bartender into letting him slip out with a bottle of beer to drink on the short drive to one of LA's second rate strip clubs. Since they are more or less free of prostitution his money will be more or less safe from a full frontal assault during a moment of weakness. He'll also stop for a half-pint. They don't serve alcohol in California clubs that feature total nudity. To him this annoyance is a typically compromising guess by a legislative body fearlessly striking out at a cause that could never strike back with a credible lobby. Pussy and potables don't mix, at least not the overt kind. That sort of entertainment requires a clear head, quick reflexes.

One pocket stocked with bourbon, the other money wise, Ben pays his seven dollars, hears all about the one *drink* minimum, and enters the club. No sooner does he wiggle into the spacious and comfortable seating next to the lavish and ornate stage, than he is attended to by one of the courteous and helpful *cocktail* waitresses.

"There's a one drink minimum per show. I hope you saw the sign when you came in. Anyway, they're supposed to tell you. What do you want," says a swimsuit clad girl—one piece, but it's a small, oddly shaped piece—holding a small tray.

"Yes, I heard," says Ben. "That's no problem. What are my choices?"

The girl sighs. Why is her life plagued with ignorant dolts? "Everything's three-fifty and there's no alcohol," she says.

"Okay, but what do you have?" he says.

"No alcohol. You gotta get something else, and it's three-fifty. Now what do you want?" She is making it clear that she is irked and can't be expected to stand around waiting forever for this guy to figure it out.

He tries, "What do you think I should get?"

This is almost too much, now the jerk can't make up his mind. She gives him what she imagines is her most intimidating look and slowly pronounces, "Non-alcoholic malt beverage, orange soda, coffee, sparkling apple cider, water. One drink minimum per show. Everything is three-fifty. Tell me what you want or I'll eighty-six you."

"Water. I'll have water, please," he says. "And just how much is it for you to eighty-six me?"

She walks away without responding. She is moving slowly, but her speed picks up as soon as she gets the word *water* written down on a napkin.

As he waits for her return, he watches a naked girl on the

stage. Legs spread and knees in air, she grinds out a message to another patron who sits opposite Ben. With great ceremony the man places a dollar bill on the edge of the stage, fixes his gaze between the dancers wide open legs, and winks at her pussy. On the corner to his left another man scribbles nervously on a napkin. Watching this, Ben's about ready for a slug of bourbon in the rest room, but he wants to pay the waitress first and avoid any further difficulty. He doesn't want to be eighty-sixed.

She returns carrying a styrofoam cup, into which she splashes some water from a ten ounce bottle. She puts the dripping bottle and cup on the counter in front of him.

"Three-fifty," she says, staring not at Ben but at whatever might be occupying the space five inches above his left ear.

"Could I have fives, please," he says, placing a one hundred dollar bill on her tray. This is his way of asserting himself at a strip club. He is making it known that he will be tipping with five dollar bills instead of the ubiquitous singles that are stacked in front of the other customers. Often he is outdone by some guy using twenties or even hundreds, but that's overkill. All he needs to do is to distinguish himself from the crowd. He'll be attended to as well as the really big suckers now. At the most he'll drop eighty or ninety bucks, small price to pay for a room full of two-minute girlfriends. It is his ugly masculinity surfacing in an environment that loves to entertain such folly. He is buying their attention. They will all pretend to like him now. "Keep one for yourself," he says absently as he watches the dancer.

The waitress says nothing but is pleasantly surprised. She has already pegged Ben as an asshole, and as she walks away, she applauds herself on her perception. Ben looks after her swimsuit covered little frame. She is small, less than five feet, tiny and cute with no substance, an appetizer. The other girls are looking at him as the small one reaches the group for the tag. They bend to listen and then smile at his caught eye. He ambles into the bathroom, thinks about jerking off, downs his bourbon, and returns to his seat. A different dancer is on the stage and his fives are next to his drink. The waitress, who has been standing guard, raises her eyebrows at him in acknowledgement of his return and twirls away.

He turns his attention to the dancer on stage, or, more accurately, to her reflection in the giant mirror-covered wall on the side of the stage. Tall and blond, the reflection dances as much for its more tangible partner as for the roomful of hopelessly average men sipping orange soda. To him there is nothing more beautiful than the relationship between the reflection of a woman and the woman who creates it. The opportunity to stare at this phenomenon is the best part of a strip club, for even these hardened exhibitionists, these visual prostitutes, cannot escape betraying their fascination with themselves. He sees exposed a self-communication far beyond superficial hope and disappointment, and close to contentment. When they look at their own images they become nothing but vulnerable; they touch reality, and it is that moment which sends through him a shot of electricity, inspires him with an oh, so temporary knowledge of humanity. At least this is how it seems to him; this is his view. And when, having collected their tips from the railing and floor of the stage, they kiss his cheek and thank him, he feels closer to them. And if their kiss lingers or if he thinks it might have lingered, he falls, for a drunken moment, truly in love with them.

The dancer turns her back on the crowd, and with her hips swaying to the music, faces fully an electric fan on the corner of the stage. Eyes closed, she indulges in the fast moving air. The sweat glistens on her face, drips along little trails down her back, shines on her buttocks. Wildly blowing hair is thrown about in a blur as she spins and mounts the vertical mirror. Head down now, legs spread, feet straddled, and hands stretched high above, she presses herself against her reflection and grinds out the rhythm of sex. She turns and struts back to the front of the stage. The glass no longer holds the reflection, but on its surface remain her two hand prints. There they will stay for the rest of the show. They will hang silently in the background as the other dancers perform, one after another. Ben will look back and see them as he leaves for glasses yet unemptied. They will be there all through the night as the club sits in stillness. Then they will be wiped away by the small Korean cleaning man who maintains his survival through the wielding of torn rags and dented buckets. He'll dutifully clean away the hand prints, having never seen the reflection.

Later, out on the street, blood running high with adventure and thin with bourbon, Ben decides to get laid. Naturally, since he lacks both the skill and the inclination to pursue a socially acceptable sex act, this means finding a hooker. As attractive as he must be to women, drunken and slurring and slobbering all over them, they just don't seem interested in him. Actually, they usually are at first, and he suspects that they would be later, but there's that unsightly hump of getting acquainted that neither he nor they can quite get over. Anyway, to him there's no better meshing of social and biological functions than paid sex. It's always gratifying, leaving him quite pleased with himself and with the world in general. He is amused by men who proudly proclaim that they *have never paid for it*. This remark, so unnecessarily spoken yet spoken out of great necessity to the speaker, indicates to Ben that these guys are either completely superficial, or strongly homosexual and running scared, or... what? Why must they assert this, and always using the exact same phrase? Unless of course they're stating that money is more sacred to them than sex, a position that would truly separate a man from his species.

Paid sex isn't as free as it used to be; it has become a virtual moral casualty of law enforcement's circuitous efforts against related violent crimes. So Ben is not sure where to go to find a street hooker these days. There is a house on the Westside that he used to frequent, but he doesn't want to spend that kind of money, especially now that his income has all come in and is really fixed. He gets into his car and heads for the low rent districts— bop popping on a budget—where he used to go and where they used to be. Stopping at a liquor store he buys a can of budget malt liquor, just to keep up the spirit of tonight's continuing drama. At times like this he likes to think of his life as one big piece of performance art. Not structured enough to be an actual play, it is full of irrationality and minuscule details and can only be viewed from the inside out. Once. By him. If he doesn't black out. He titles this episode: Pinching pennies and prostitutes—frugal fucking in LA.

Arriving way down on the east end of Sunset he points his car west and begins driving slowly, at the speed limit, in the right lane. This is different from real driving, as he is not trying to get anywhere. It's more like sitting in your car and observing the passing sights while the planet rotates underneath. He loves this part of town, loves the fact that there are people here who would gladly slit his throat for the money in his pocket, something to keep in mind in case he decides to hire the work out. He feels somehow close to these people, but at the same time he knows that they despise him from the word go, because whatever he is—they don't know, and that doesn't matter—it is what they cannot be. The oppressive air hangs still above the street and seems to sweat the inexhaustible supply of perennial refuse that surrounds and infiltrates every scene. The filth of the road is blown on to the sidewalk, from there pushed against the buildings, finally coming to its semi-permanent resting place under ledges and in doorframes of abandoned businesses. Empty wine bottles wearing paper bags and newspaper circulars telling stories about produce and canned spaghetti serve as the makings of a disposable bed for disposable humans. Doors that would pass for nailed shut open briefly and spit out black men wearing leather blazers and berets who stoop at the passenger window of a waiting Cadillac; a moment later the car pulls away. Bob's Lucky Stop Liquor No. 6 is shutting down for the night. A Korean man, presumably Bob, pulls along an iron track the first of three black accordion security gates that, when closed, go nicely with similar iron that covers the display window. Painted on its glass, behind the bars, is a smiling blond dressed in black velvet and holding a glass of whiskey: Ben's dream: prisoner of a liquor store. So far there are no women for hire, but then he's still too far east; perhaps closer to Western. He drives on.

Normandie, Winoa, Kingsley, Harvard, Hobart, Serrano, and Western, were once a great Hollywood district bounteous with girls at the peak of their powers who traded in pussies and tongues and lived the prime of their lives in a lightning flash, witnessing the brief rise and fall of their street values pass in the space of a few short years. Now it is populated by desperate women, far fewer in number, and leading much harder and shorter lives, heroines of subsistence in service of whoremaster heroin, this world not yet cracked. But even these dying embers are not visible to Ben as he scans from left side to road to right side to road. Smooth, observational, and moving at a nearly constant twenty-five miles per hour, he and his car glide through the green light at Western and Sunset and slip properly into the heart of Hollywood.

On the top of the steering wheel rests his left hand, and around the third finger of his hand is wrapped a gold wedding band. Rendered barren of its original significance, it is the only tangible relic of a marriage long gone by. Two years earlier he had

removed it, having finally convinced a girl that still wanted to
believe in him that he was indeed of no value to anyone, least of
all to her, and certainly not to himself. They parted with no
malice, she regretful, he drunk. His initial infatuation with
blameless drinking and womanizing quickly wore thin as things
settled back into the downward spiral that he had become accustomed to; settled back, in fact, with no delay and no surprise to
him. He has never deciphered what was the chicken and what was
the egg; his drinking encouraged her resentment and her resentment accelerated his drinking. Given the choice, he prefers
sucking vodka to thinking about it, her. A month ago, as the full
horror of his situation and found intentions began to fascinate
him, he took to wearing the ring again. Now it clicks lightly on the
wheel as his finger absently hops up and down, and his car
continues to roll down Sunset. Wilton, Van Ness, Bronson,
Tamarind, still a fruitless search: no more proffered apples.

He spots a girl peeking around a corner, but when he pulls to
the side and slows, leaning towards the passenger window and
beckoning her, she flees. He is at Gower and decides to stop at one
of the crusty little bars in that area, where John Steinbeck once
drank, or so Ben has read. He gets inside just in time for last call.
The lateness of the hour has taken him by surprise—very unusual—and he can relax only with the knowledge that back at
home he is adequately stocked for the night. The inconvenience
of having to keep track of time is steadily growing as his inclination and even his ability to do so diminishes. It is probably too late
for a Sunset date, but intent on continuing the search he talks the
bartender into pouring two glasses of iced vodka which he downs
directly. He leaves the bar as the lights go up and returns to his car.
As this new alcohol enters his blood, he and his dark designs slip
back into the ever heavy flow of traffic. Vine, Morningside,
Cahuenga through Highland, and then Hollywood High-land on

to La Brea; not until he arrives at the corner of Sunset and Sierra Bonita does he see the girl that he will pay to fuck. She is a young Hispanic girl, and Ben appreciates the reasonable rhyme of her appearance with the street she has chosen to stand on.

He pulls to the curb and says, "Good evening."

Before meeting his eyes she cautiously looks up and down the street. Satisfied that they are not being watched she approaches his car and, hands on knees, bends to the window.

"You wanna date? You wanna date me?" she says.

Her eyes never stop moving. She looks at Ben, then to her left, then at his lap, then across the street, then at his feet. She seems to digest everything she looks at in one quick glance, so that when she looks again it is not because she wants to see more but because she wants to see the same thing *now*, to see if her original information needs to be updated.

Ben knows that she knows that he is not a cop, and he is somewhat amused at her defensive manner: a caged rat that repeatedly reenters the cage. Willing to shoulder the legal exposure and hopefully put her at ease, he turns over some of his cards.

"I'll give you a hundred dollars for a straight forty-five minutes. You get the room," he says. Then, because he can never resist the poetry of completion, he shows her the money, thereby either tempting her assent or tightening his own noose.

Her eyes grab the money, then let go. "The room is twenty. You pay for it," she says, not because she wouldn't, but because she thinks that he will.

Normally this would prompt him to split. He made a good clean offer and now he's being sucked on. "Okay," he says, not because it is, but because he suddenly feels that a surrender here will fit nicely into the big picture.

The motel is just across the street; he'll park on a side street and meet her by the office. But when he steps out of the car and stands upright he is struck with a wave of alcohol that has been building in his seated body. Vodka on ice is nice. When he reaches his whore he is much drunker than he'd like to be and too drunk to realize it: less control, right where he needs it most.

♣    ♣    ♣

He awakens on the floor of his apartment, just inside the door, ten miles and six hours away from his last memory. Springing to his knees he checks for his wallet. It is in his pocket and still contains the forty-four one hundred dollar bills that he stuffed into it at the bar. Pausing on all fours, he stares at the floor as if to read his next direction there. He manages to get to his feet and open the door. Miraculously, but not surprisingly, his car is parked soundly on the street. This was too much, too far to drive in a blackout. He can only hope that he didn't hurt anyone while driving home, but he's pretty sure that if he had it would have already come to him in a rush of nausea and spectacular recollection. For further confirmation he staggers out to the car; it bears no scars, and he relaxes. He goes back inside for a drink and to sit down and try to reconstruct what happened with the hooker.

As he sits at the kitchen table, tentatively gulping vodka and whatever-was-in-the-fridge, random memories of the night before flash in and out of his head. With no respect for chronology they are like a slide show at a stranger's house, the box of slides having been dropped and hastily reassembled just before presentation. He is always very uncomfortable with these absences of palpable participation in his own life, and the fact that they are increasing in both intensity and frequency makes him long to be anonymous. Never considering a backward step, he thinks only of Las Vegas and how it is clearly time to go there. He won't feel right today until he can establish at least an outline of last night. In the past he would call whomever he had been drinking with and ask them, or even pick up clues from his wife; for back then he was often at home in front of the television before the blackout. Now he is and was alone, and that's how he must go about remembering whatever he can. Ice clinks in his empty glass. Outside there are the sounds of morning.

He has an image of being near a garbage hopper, presumably in the rear of the motel. He has no recollection of the inside of a motel room. Pursuing that thought, he remembers the girl taking the room money from him and going to the office alone. When she returned she offered some sort of vague explanation and led him to the back of the building. Apparently his condition was not lost on her; she must have kept the room money, as his pocket is empty. In fact, after watching him dig out that twenty, she may have taken the rest of the money from his front pocket and thought that she had cleaned him out. That could be why his wallet is intact.

He has an image of leaning on dirty steel as the girl kneeled before him, his penis in her mouth. He cannot remember coming, or even having an erection.

He has an image of the girl hugging him and kissing his neck. He tried to kiss her mouth and she turned quickly. She bent to kiss his hand and started sucking on his fingers. As she fondled his penis she continued sucking his fingers.

He has an image of her pulling him by the hand as they crossed the street. She closed his car door for him. In his mirror he saw her cross the street again.

He has an image of endless driving, of a locked liquor store, of being in Inglewood and not knowing his way home.

Well, he thinks, not as bad as I thought; I remember a lot of it. He pours another drink and, now in better spirits, decides to clean up and have a few at the bar down the street. There he'll seriously think about Las Vegas: when he will leave, what to do with all his stuff. Actually, he already knows what he will do with his stuff; he just needs to work out the details.

Washing his hands, he notices that the wedding ring is missing from his finger. He pauses and looks at himself in the mirror, confirming in his mind that he should be wearing it; that is, he was wearing it last night and can't remember taking it off. As logic completes what his memory can only begin, the what-must-have-happened unfolds in his own eyes. The word *bitch* arrives at his lips, but he refrains from phonation. After all, she was just doing her job.

The perpetual cloud of alcohol wears momentarily thin, or perhaps it is just his survival instinct beating through. Either way, before leaving for the nearby bar he is struck with the realization that he hasn't eaten for quite some time—hasn't eaten substantially for even longer. Though he is not hungry, and though the very thought of solid food brings a clear and present rush of nausea to his gut, he knows that he must make a go of it, must try to eat something. If for no better reason than to extend his drinking base, to sustain the heart that pumps the blood that carries the alcohol to his brain, he seeks out nutrition.

The refrigerator abruptly clicks off its motor when he opens the door and, now awake after a long nap, yawns a breathy white mist at his face. Ben scans its interior for his options. In disuse it has remained neat and clean. Not one to let things spoil—other things—he has kept the fridge free from moldy cheese and rotten milk, free from the usual assortment of unidentified dying objects usually found in the overstocked refrigerators of happy, healthy families. It contains only a partial chocolate bar, a baked but not eaten potato which he throws in the garbage, a tub of margarine, an ice cube tray filled with water which he returns to the freezer, several bottles of gone-flat mixers and sodas, a small bag of coffee, and a green pepper purchased last week, now in the final stages of edibility. Inclined to something green he selects the pepper and, taking a gulp of vodka for courage, slices it into quarters. Discarding the shriveled areas of the vegetable, he is left with two cavernous sections; they rest alone in the center of his plate. The sweat beads on his forehead as he bites half of one of the pieces and chews. He swallows the small pulpy quantity and waits while watching for distraction a high-mileage, very beat cat run across the street. A protest begins in his outraged stomach. Reflexively he pushes away from the table and bends slightly forward. Determined not to surrender this little bit of hard won food, he stiffens in his chair and slowly blows air out of his mouth, a trick used by him in the past to successfully fight nausea in public. Painfully, white faced in his kitchen chair, he fights the good fight, and manages to keep down the bite of green pepper until the crisis passes. Then hopeful, renewed, proud of his victory, and rather sated, he tosses out the remaining food and jaunts out the door.

At the bar he settles into his barstool position and begins working on the nuts and bolts of going to Las Vegas. Having deduced the inevitability of the trip he sees no reason to delay it further. When he gets to Vegas his first act will be... his first act will be to have a drink, and his second act will be to pawn his watch. Time will be money. Hopefully, he will never again know what time it is. If he should want a drink, he need only go out and buy one—anytime, anywhere. The bartender puts his vodka down hard on the bar and collects a few bills from the little pile in front of Ben, all the time shaking his head in silent disapproval.

"I think when I'm done with this I'll have gin and tonic, Bombay gin and tonic," says Ben just to taunt him.

The bartender, unable to keep silent any longer, flares at him. "You should be having coffee! All the time in here, do you know what time it is? You're a young man. It's none of my business, but if you could see what I see you wouldn't do this to yourself."

Ben is moved. Perhaps he is being unintentionally cruel to this caring human being by making him participate in Ben's Personal Theater of Tragedy. But what happened here? This man is a bartender. Ben's a drunk. What's the problem? Tough call, the old guy's trying to show some unbridled compassion, some unconditional concern. Ben could cry here if he worked at it, so he decides to burn the bridge.

"I understand what you're saying and why you're saying it," he says to the bartender. "I appreciate your concern, and it's not my intention to make you uncomfortable. Serve me today, and I won't ever come in here again. If I do you can eighty-six me."

"Sure, sure, I can eighty-six you now if I want. Stop fucking with me. I don't give a fuck what you do." He picks up a bottle of gin and fills a glass, slamming it down angrily in front of Ben. "On the house, son," he says and knocks the bar twice with his knuckles.

Ben turns his back to the bar and sits looking at the room. He is jolted by a tug at his sleeve. Turning, he finds the image of a middle aged man whom he has seen muttering to himself on the street and sometimes in the bar. The man is making noises at Ben. Unintelligible, the sounds are similar to snorts and grunts, with the vocal cords being struck only sporadically. Figuring that this is probably a visual aid sent over by the bartender, Ben nods in sarcastic acknowledgement to the man who is indeed watching from the far end of the bar, and offers a five dollar bill to the impaired man who then shuffles away, clutching it. The scene saddens Ben, as does any encounter with hurt persons, life's victims. As he gets up to leave he feels the familiar nausea and shortness of breath. His heart is beating very fast these days, and he's not been able to give it any sort of proper fuel. He can tell already that his own body won't outlast his mind, but what if it did? That would be truly awful, he thinks, everybody thinks.

He goes directly to the liquor store and replenishes his home supply, this time with gin: a new leaf, a fresh start, a new man. He also buys a roll of heavy duty trash bags and a can of charcoal lighter, and convinces the reluctant clerk to give up as many empty liquor boxes as Ben can carry home. Ben combines the boxes as efficiently as possible inside of each other and, after putting his purchases in the innermost box, ends up with a fairly compact package. He won't need to go home for the car; he can carry his disposal kit easily in his arms.

He deals first with the generic things, things that, when scattered, will bear no reflection of him or his life. Methodically each book on his shelf is inspected for clues about its owner, a handwritten name: *If found, return to...*, a penned inscription: *With love to Ben, who has always enjoyed Fuk-en-her.*, or a shopping list, a note, forgotten by his wife: *grapefruit, six-pack or sale twelve, chicken + ? OK?—call B.* These details, when found, are removed and the book packed neatly in a box. Pans, lamps, old clothes, things that are usable but have limited value are boxed with the books. Boxes run out and bags take over. Desk accessories, tools, a phone, a vacuum cleaner, an old television— like the Grinch stealing Christmas, Ben stuffs the bulk of his belongings into jumbo plastic trash bags and stuffs the bags into his car. Trip by trip, hour by hour, he delivers his ex-stuff to local organizations. Goodwill gets some, a Venice halfway house re-ceives kitchen utensils and a TV, men wandering the boardwalk are enriched with clothes and canned food to add to their already overloaded shopping carts, an acquaintance down the street scores a stereo and a quick explanation that Ben is leaving town in a hurry to take a new job in Denver. Ben labors into the night, glass at his side and refreshed by his own industriousness. Bags are left outside the gates of closed charities. A neighbor boy sleeps, unaware that he is now the owner of a slightly used French ten speed bicycle which, newly polished, sits bearing a note on the back porch. On and on, he works as much out of compulsion as out of thoughtfulness, for he cannot bear to see waste, much less generate it. Also, his cause is well served. So separated from him and each other, his possessions no longer have a story to tell. They are reduced to elements, building blocks of a modern American existence. No longer parts summing into a whole, they are without collective meaning, an eraser mark on the page of his life.

His energy is there for him, running with him, high and constant. For him there is a grim thrill in this crystallization of intent. Just as a woman will break an engagement by returning the ring, it is this activity, this thing to be done, that is calling together for Ben all his recent meandering. Motion, long absent and now that much more refreshing, motion toward his future is what he is generating. The rush is tangible and of such intensity so as to preclude abstract considerations of backward and forward, to and from, growth and death. These terms are not of the moment; arguably, they are not of any moment. This tapestry which he is unraveling never really told a story to begin with; it was always non-figurative and woven without volition.

Very drunk, but well fueled with purpose, he turns to the more detailed task of purging the very personal things. He builds a small fire in the brazier on his patio. In goes the amateur artwork. that he has created: the photographs, a carved piece of pine, a watercolor painted over a love poem to his wife, a story he had written. In goes his file drawer: the medical records, the ten-forty copies, the car repair receipts, the warranties, the birth and marriage certificates. In goes the scrapbook: the polaroids of parties, the postcards from Hawaii, the totem-pole-esque strips of vending machine photos carried away from arcades and fairs. He scoops out the accumulated debris and ashes; then, using char-coal lighter, and in an effort not so much to destroy as to ruin, to render worthless, he tosses into the flames those things that he will not keep, but doesn't want anyone else to possess: his camera, his motorcycle jacket, his wife's left-behind clothes, a clock purchased in Paris, a rosewood cigar box crafted by his father, a pair of binoculars brought away from World War Two by his grandfather, his engraved stationery, gifts with too much mean-ing to live on without him, purchased art that he can finally possess only by effecting its destruction. More cleaning of ashes, then it burns on—a fire in the gestalt. He works, it burns, until the task is done and the fire itself is gone.

It is morning. He calls his landlord: he will be out of the apartment by the end of the month, big new job in Denver. He's sorry about the short notice, but he won't be needing his security deposit back. The place will be clean, but would it be okay if he left behind a few pieces of furniture? He's sure that the balance due him will more than cover the cost of having it hauled away. He's grateful for everything and wishes good luck. A loose end is tied.

Apart from his bed and some heavy furniture, what remains, what he owns, what's left, fits into a suitcase. Ben looks around himself, surveying the apartment. The job has been well done. How right, he thinks, that what I have done so well here is to undo. And indeed, he continues to be a tireless architect of his own undoing.

After a nap he decides on a late lunch of gin and an apple, which seems to go down more easily than vodka and a green pepper did; he is able to eat two sections of the apple. Though there is no longer any reason for him to stay in Los Angeles—he has long since forsaken any friends that he may have had here—he is still reluctant, almost apprehensive, to leave for Las Vegas. It may be simply that he knows that the five hour drive, once just

JOHN O'BRIEN

an overgrown commute to him, will be difficult if not hellish in his present condition. More likely he is experiencing an unaddressed second thought, irrational anxiety born from his cognizance that this is to be a one way trip, and if he can avoid the final journey he can avoid the final destination. But in fact he is already well along on this trip, and going to Las Vegas is merely kindling a fire that is even now raging. He will go soon, he wants to. Tonight is here however, and so he cleans up and heads out for the bars. In the mood to pay four and five dollars for each drink, he has donned his suit. He finds nothing more entertaining than bars in over-priced chichi restaurants. A lone alcoholic, albeit well-dressed and formerly good-looking, he will embarrass the rude staff and intrigue the young girls who are always in search of cocaine and Porsches.

And so he finds himself at such a place in Malibu. After the breezy drive up the coast he is ready for this, his last night in LA. He has never been to this place, and the white smocked bartenders have never seen him. He is grateful to sit and drink anonymously; he will enjoy this aspect of Vegas. There was a time when he nurtured his stature as a *regular* in bars all over Los Angeles. He would make special trips out to bars that he had been away from simply to reaffirm his familiarity. He enjoyed being called by name, having his drink order predicted, or at least guessed at. But now he is known to those places as a pathetic drunk. Like the incident at the bar in Venice, he must now endure judgment as part of his bar tab. They hate to see him. They roll their eyes. They shake their heads. Serving him has become a moral question for bartenders that once poured liquor into his glass freely. *On me!* they would exclaim, and marvel at his ability to drink enormous quantities and never give a hint of intoxication. He was a star. Now he is a case.

It is early in the evening. He is still riding a wave of purpose and has the extra internal energy to prove it. His head is not yet drooping. He doesn't appear to be brooding over his drink. So, if one can look past the bloated condition of his face, Ben looks okay, even rather dashing, sitting confidently at the marble bar, looking like someone who knows what he's doing, like someone who is bearing up under unreasonable pain. This vision is not lost on an attractive woman in her thirties who has entered the bar alone and taken a seat on the opposite side from Ben. She watches him through a jungle of chrome-spouted bottles, hoping to catch his eye. When she does, realizing that this may be her only communication with him, she gives him a meaningful, somehow profound smile.

It is a remarkable smile, extremely familiar but without a trace of professionalism, and Ben wonders at its intensity. It is a touch, a piece of communication. The smile she gives to him is a daring embrace. It pleads for an answer. It is a gamble. It is an affirmation of humanity. It is a sympathetic speech that is intended to cut through the fact of where they are and suggest where they could be. It says: *You may be able to save my life, I know that I can save yours.* It says: *I know that you know me, I know you.* It is shrouded in abysmal despair, and yet remains hopeful. It is an assertion of strength; it craves but does not need. Ben comprehends it all, yet finds himself unable to respond. Locked in a circle of logical inaccessibility, he thinks: I am not good enough to be with you, and because I will not be with you, I am not good enough. His gaze instantly assumes a downward cant. The girl, having not yet received her order, leaves. Too much has transpired. The bartender, holding her drink, looks around the room for her. Ben calls him over and explains that the girl, a friend of his, had to leave suddenly. Ben pays for her drink.

In the face of this further confirmation of his inability to perform a function, to have a value, he swings moodily down-

ward. An angel from *the city of…* came to see him on his last
night in her town, and all he could do was look at his glass. The
evening's adventure has been pretty much ruined, for he was just
offered the grand prize, and he turned away. Given that, what
exactly should he be looking forward to? He doubts that even a
cheerful chat with Camus, an existential pep talk, could inspire
him to endure this particular absurdity.

Having properly set himself up now, he plunges wildly back
into his liquor, ordering and reordering at a feverish pace, and
drinking a quantity that is unusually high, even for him. He finds
himself buying rounds for brief acquaintances at the bar, who
down them quickly and move along to dinner or to another seat
though they are not quite sure what it is about him that has
frightened them. Despite all that he is consuming he is keeping to
the right of the line and not becoming overtly obnoxious. Tonight
is plastic night and he wants everyone to share the wealth. He will
discreetly inebriate LA; it will be his going away party. When he
senses people noticing his behavior at one bar, he simply signs the
invoice and drives down the road to another. Amused, he thinks
that this may be how they ultimately find his corpse, a trail of
American Express charges leading right up to the final room
service bottle of bourbon clutched in one stiff fist, his heart in the
other. Even in his death, no doubt, he will haunt Amex, causing
them to be charged the additional fees incurred in getting his
rotting stink out of the hotel room. Tonight he has many stops to
make before going home, and home is the last stop before Vegas.
Tomorrow he will move away from his mailbox, and since he has
always been so meticulous about paying his bill in the past,
American Express won't even think twice about a couple of
months without a payment. He'll be wearing a tag on his toe long
before the first computer-generated letters start arriving at his

last known address. Bar after bar, the rooms fade into each other, and all turn eventually into sand, as he loses his grip and blacks out.

♣   ♣   ♣

He awakens on a hard cold floor; it is wet. His eyes see only white. As consciousness returns, more or less fully, he realizes that he is on the floor of a public rest room, his head in a urinal. There is sand on the floor, and looking around, he sees that it is one of the public beach rest rooms. Very nice. Sitting up he finds himself still in one piece, unmolested and unrobbed; in any case, his big money is safe at home. Stiffly he stands. He rinses his mouth and splashes his face. Outside, the recently risen sun reveals his car, alone in a parking lot about a hundred yards away. The keys are in his pocket, along with a wad of blue American Express receipts. He is amazed at how well he is taking this. A year ago, if he had found himself sleeping in a urinal, he probably would have committed suicide on the spot—death by grossness. Instead he goes back into the rest room and cleans up as well as he can. He recognized a restaurant up on the road; he is just south of Malibu.

He gets up to his car and pulls out onto the coast highway. He'll head for home, to shower and rest and get his stuff, and then drive to Las Vegas. He makes a mental note to call ahead and get a room, as he'll no doubt need a bed as soon as he hits town. A bed, not a urinal, he thinks, that sort of thing has got to stop before it gets worse... worse? First he needs a drink. It is early so, thinking that he will have to make do with a six-pack for now, he looks for a market. But apparently his luck is holding; he sees a bona fide fully liquor-licensed restaurant that is serving breakfast. The banner reads: *Hair-of-the-shark special. Two eggs, Two strips of*

*bacon, Two pieces of toast, and Two marys, screws, or hounds.*
*Your choice.* Bloody marys, screwdrivers, or greyhounds—
breakfast of carrion, he thinks, pulling into the lot.

"Hi. Have you had a chance to look at the menu?" says a
bouncy young ponytailed girl, pencil at the ready. Ben is seated
on the sunny patio, and the waitress is politely ignoring the fact
that he is, at best, disheveled.

He envies her seemingly happy life, her willingness to stay
ignorant of his miserable condition. He keeps getting whiffs of
urine from, he guesses, his own face, and hopes she doesn't notice;
but again, he's not as mortified about it as he ought to be. Perhaps
this is how the mind starts going. An early warning sign of mental
illness: the subject readily accepts the odor of piss on his own face.

"Good Morning," he says, "I would like a piece of dry white
toast and two double Bombay-tonics, please." He awaits her
reaction. Inside he feels anxiety rearing its nasty little head. He
knows that he is still well-loaded from last night, but just the same
its time for more. Now.

"That's all?" she asks, getting it all down. Surprisingly, she is
not surprised. Perhaps she is not as young as she looks.

"That's it for now," he says. "Oh, you do take American
Express here, right?"

"Yes sir, sure do." For some reason, she beams with this
information. "But there is a ten dollar minimum."

"No problem," he says, urine assailing his nostrils. "Could
you point me to the rest room? I've had a little accident."

She picks up his menu. "Right down there," she says, pointing.

He gets up, and with difficulty, walks. The rich odor from the
coffee machine reaches him and momentarily replaces the foul
smells of his night. He hears a sea gull scream, feels a cool ocean
breeze. He already misses Los Angeles, the whole fucking place.

lemons

Her first sensation is th
Her bed is saturated
that it could be wrung

# irst; then she feels wet. with sweat, so much from the sheets, and it

has grown cold and terribly uncomfortable during the night. It is her sweat, and though she hates the way it feels, against and alienated from her skin, she remains where she is, staring at the ceiling and vaguely wondering why the cracks in the plaster no longer bother her. Al, her old and new lover, occupies the place next to her. Still asleep, the expression on his face is one of garlic aplomb. His eyes are deep in their sockets, as if in retreat from too many miles witnessed. Sera's eyes do not move; her mouth is dry and open. The bed is cold, wet, and fucked-up, and she wonders if it isn't time to get out of it; indeed, the sun is already stale in the sky.

Awakening two hours later, Al finds her lying next to him. The wetness of the bed delivers its message to him, and he secretly revels in the fact that he can still create this much terror in her. Safely on his target, he now admits to himself his recent doubts about his power over her. Clearly it continues to exist; she remains his possession.

"I missed you, Sera. You have been lonely," he says, master of the assertive question.

She blinks and turns her head to him—two motions. "I'm older now, Al."

"But still a flower. Why such a little home? Why such a little life?" He slides his hand under the sheet and grasps firmly between her legs, his large hand easily encompassing her, meeting neither resistance nor acceptance. "You have been lonely."

Suddenly the cracked plaster on the ceiling makes sense. She *has* been lonely. His voice makes sense. This voice from so long ago—she was so young and clean then, had never been bruised—makes sense, could almost be soothing. She feels so many blanks, so many vacant strings of thought. "I've been all right," she says.

"You don't look like you have been all right, flower. You have bruises on your face. I'm sorry I wasn't there to protect you. I have been trying to keep an eye on you for the last week, but I also had other business. This will not happen again. I will keep you safe." He rolls to her side and whispers, "We are both older. You have been lonely."

The flow of sweat resumes; she has never been so thirsty. "I am lonely, Al."

"Yes," he says, mounting her, "so am I." And later: "I am very hungry, Sera. We must discuss things as you make my breakfast."

Sera expressionless and Al indifferent, they sit at her little table and eat, he more than she; in fact, she not at all.

"I cannot stay here with you, Sera. At least not until you find a larger apartment. We will have the money—you know how much money I can bring you—and we will find a big apartment…

no, a condominium! I like it here in Las Vegas. I have not been here for years—since before I knew you. But I like it. I think we can make a fortune again here." Taking a bite of food, he smiles hungrily at her. "You are sly! You knew all along that there was money here, didn't you?" Protracted, pensive chewing, a swallow, then: "Why else would you have run away."

She tenses and looks down at her cold food. *Will he hurt me now?*

As before in the bed, he can smell her fear, and it is enough. This is all he needs, just a little confirmation. He laughs, "No... I told you that you have nothing to fear from me. Just accept me, Sera. We belong together."

Not knowing what else to do, she nods. She thinks to smile, and does that; she used to do that a lot. Apart from these little gestures, she has no idea what to do or how to behave. She decides to sit still and wait for his cue. Beyond that it's just fog.

"What I wish to tell you is this: I must move into one of the hotels—temporarily, of course. I need some time to establish new contacts for us. Also, you can see that these are not the sort of surroundings I am accustomed to. You know, I truly belong in wealth and luxury. You will call this morning and find a suite for me in one of the tall buildings. Perhaps the Sahara would be best. I remember it from my last trip. It is not the mockery that some of the newer hotels are."

Momentarily confused, she asks, "Where have you been staying?"

He drops his fork. "With an old friend," he tells her. "That is none of your affair."

A hole appears in the fog, small and really only a logical tiptoe away. "You'll need some money then," she says.

He measures his anger. It is still very soon, and he has been away for a long time. "It is, after all, Sera, my money."

"Yes, of course it is, Al," she says as she rises to fetch it. "How much do you want?"

"All of it. I need some clothes and things. I will try to line up some things after I check into my suite, but it will take time, and we may have to work a bar tonight. Maybe you should work the street. I have been watching you. You have a place that you like. You can go there if I am busy."

*Clothes and things?* She steps closer to him. One. Two.

Pressure. Al hates this scrutiny. It is not as it used to be, he thinks. Enough is enough. "What are you looking at," he screams, slamming his fist on the table and causing his plate to rattle threateningly, but not overturn.

"Where's all your jewelry, Al?" she asks, but by now she has guessed the answer, even before the emerald of his one remaining ring tears the still-bruised flesh of her cheek. She tumbles back against the refrigerator and crumples to the floor.

With surprisingly weak knees, Al sits down. He is trembling, and is disconcerted to find that it is not out of anger. He dare not rise to help her, but rather, sits at the table and watches her stillness. Indeed, they are both older.

♣   ♣   ♣

Early in the evening as she prepares for whatever it is that Al will ask her to do, Sera once again finds herself on both sides of her mirror. In addition to a persistent headache, Al's backhand imparted a message to her in the form of a laceration on her cheekbone. Over the last decade her flesh has taken enough abuse for her to know that this cut will never completely heal. There will be a small white scar here that will last until the day comes for it to disappear into the depths of a wrinkle, the first ever permanent infliction to be borne on her face. It establishes itself amidst her beauty even now, as the bruise beneath it, leftover from her misfortune with the three boys, labors confusedly at the final stages of healing.

But the scar is not the message; it is merely the messenger. Unlike the light, constant of speed as it paints and repaints the image before her, her thoughts are slowing, deteriorating as she sits by, the helpless spectator. Part of her wants to be detached, but a deeper, more elemental part cannot be. The fat man at the Hilton, though merely Al's instrument, was a much harder trick than even the misdirected boys of earlier in the week. She can't seem to fix this one, and she's not sure that she even cares. There is a difference, but she doesn't know what it is. Something is missing that was here before, but she doesn't know what it is.

She cries—a privilege of being alone in her room—and a saline tear stings the cut of her cheek as it washes by, taking with it a partial coating of flesh-colored powder which she was hoping might help to hide the wound. Thus laden, the tear falls from her chin and onto her panties, where it is swallowed by black lace. All is well about this, for the panties might easily have been white lace, and the tear more of a provocation.

Fully dressed, Sera tires of the mirror and goes instead to the living room to wait for Al's call. Here she turns on the television and watches not the screen, but the lambency it creates on an opposing wall. It is the stuff that dreams are made of, so with the volume off and the silence in the apartment unbroken by the phone, she falls asleep for the duration of the night.

♣    ♣    ♣

"So now I have an excuse," says Al to no one in particular. Sitting alone in his malfunctioning Mercedes on the shoulder of route 93/ 95, he is on the tail end of a temper tantrum and the calm in his own voice irks him. "I don't need one!" he shouts, banging on the steering wheel. "I don't need this excuse! What do I care of her waiting. It will build her character. She will not dare to disappoint me again!"

He is doubly frustrated because he can imagine no way to blame the failure of his car on Sera. He failed to phone her with instructions last night, though he had told her to wait for his call. Occupied with shopping yesterday evening, he was unable to arrange anything even at the bar of his hotel; then it was too late and he couldn't bring himself to admit failure to her. He needs time. He needs his jewelry back too, and this was to be his early morning errand, followed by a triumphant return with fully dressed fingers to her apartment, until the Mercedes took a piece of fuel tank rust about the size of a small kidney stone into its filterless fuel line and tried passing it through a carburetor: no go. These matters of automotive arcana are of course inscrutable to Al, who knows only that he has been dealt yet another bust card, and that the rich deck of his youth is getting harder and harder to cut; especially now that he can almost taste it, after so many hard, private years.

And what could be more descriptive of his life than this car. Taken by him as payment of a should-have-been-forgotten debt from an aging Venezuelan drug wholesaler who had to flee Canada—*flee Canada!*—and who found himself, on one unfortunate afternoon, in the same plasma clinic on Sunset Boulevard that was frequented by Al. Al left that clinic with a set of car keys and about as much legal ownership of the yellow Mercedes as the man from whom he had taken it had had. Earlier possessorship of the car is sketchy, but it is probable that the serial number had long since faded from any official silicon, which it certainly must have at one time occupied. Though it pained him to squander his blood money, Al could not bear to drive such an unclean car, but it was the true color of the Mercedes, as it emerged from the wet, fluorescent tunnel of Suds-N-Spray out into the daylight, that really caused him to stop and solemnly mourn the great black beasts of his long-gone wealth.

And the fall had been swift and certain, though Al could not in a million years explain what happened, or at least was not able to explain it to himself in six years. It could have been any or all of the myriad influences which converged on him virtually simultaneously. Sera left. Then two other girls left, Then Hollywood got super dry—no new girls, no old girls, nothing. Then he tried to move some drugs and got busted for the first time in his life. Then it seemed he got busted all the time, for anything. Then his attorney sued him, and all his property was seized. Then came the immigration problems from out of the blue. Then he was totally alone and had nothing.

After all the different things had happened, they looked to him, in his mind's eye, more like just one big thing, something that he could overcome. So, rather than be not-Al, he stayed and did everything he knew to do to become Al again. But he couldn't. Then he got old—again, all at once. Like a tumor, a thought had been growing, perennial and torpid, in the back of his mind. There was something that he had defeated long ago; it was away, in a different place, and for that reason, he thought, he could defeat it again. It had been a big thing in his life. Now it was greatly distant from his life, and it didn't even know that he knew where it was.

A lesson that Al took away from Los Angeles is: do what must be done, so he gives up on retrieving his pawned jewelry today and starts off on foot down the road to a gas station which is visible in the distance and somehow looks expensive.

But the fact that he does this doesn't change the way he feels about doing it. Al hates this, and the anger that rages inside his head is splenetic and bleak. He hates the fact that he is walking on the side of a desert highway so that he can overpay a disgusting American grease monkey to fix a hideous piss-colored wreck, all so he can go and humiliate himself in front of Sera—who has never been all that blind, he knows—by demanding more money with which he can secretly get his jewelry back from a pawnbroker! This is not what Gamal Fathi's destiny is meant to be, and there can be little doubt that the blame should be placed on... on the evil American forces that have all along conspired to make his life a living hell, on the cesspool that is Los Angeles, on the faithless and disloyal women to whom he has offered only kindness and protection. He wants for so little in comparison to those fattened corporate Americans who once came to him with their repellent requests and whose greed is limitless. Perhaps it is they who are responsible; perhaps it is everyone, for what non-collective power could paint his soul with so much acrimony, so much venom.

♣ ♣ ♣

Sera has been awake for hours, watching the silent television, which as she slept drifted in and out of a three-hour test pattern. The absence of sound does little to alter the inanity of daytime TV, but this is not an observation that she is capable of making right now; it is far too irrelevant and would undermine her fascination in the image of a man soundlessly screaming as a superimposed *$10,000* burns on his chest.

Hungry. She's pretty sure that she ought to eat, but the kitchen isn't holding much this morning. So... what? Yes, she generally goes out to the store at a time like this, but she dare not. Al would be very angry indeed if he called or came over and she wasn't here. There's an enormous distraction here. If she had enough money she could go play blackjack. But she really can't leave. She can eat later. She could use a trick—go back to work. Al will find her something. On the television is a local commercial: the power company wants her and her family to know more about the Hoover Dam. She knows, she's heard the copy many times this week. An aerial shot of a rushing river dissolves to a very still Lake Mead, then the dam, looking about seven hundred and twenty-six feet tall, if she remembers correctly. She should check her makeup. She goes to the bedroom and checks her makeup.

From the bedroom she hears—she forgot to lock the door—the sound of her front door opening.

"Sera." Al's voice booms from the other room.

"Al. I'm here in my bedroom, Al. I'm hungry."

Taken aback for no apparent reason, Al stops, still in the other room, and cocks his head. Too many problems this morning, or maybe he's just hungry too. Ultimately, after catching his own reflection in an oblique window, he smiles broadly at her tone. Probably best, he thinks, not even to mention his failure to call last night.

Entering her bedroom, he finds her at her mirror waiting expectantly, and says, "Then I shall buy you lunch. You will need your strength tonight. After lunch we will come back here and you can shower and dress... you look a little rumpled."

"All right, Al. Let's have lunch. Then I can shower and dress," she says.

♣   ♣   ♣

Not a bad little suite, this here at the Sahara. Or is it a big room? It's sort of a sweetroom, strange American, Las Vegas, not-yet-or-no-longer-big-time type configuration. To Al, alone and waiting for Sera this late evening, it's a guess crossed with a necessary compromise. Way back at his best there was too much money spent to prevent and too much worry about people laughing at him; nobody's fool, he always suspected this, just to be on the safe side. After that, at his worst, there was no money to spend and people were definitely laughing at him. Now there's a little money, he's spending all of it, and nobody's paying any attention to him. The sweetroom here at the Sahara—wet bar with executive wood-grain refrigerator, dining alcove, two bathroom sinks—is... okay.

Too, that long gone serendipity may be returning to him, for he was able to dig up a pretty good trick for Sera tonight. Not easy—after wasting time in three different bars he finally scored all the way down at the Sands, only to discover that the guy was staying right here at the Sahara—but it all worked out. She's there now, just four floors down, with this guy and his wife. Classic work, almost like it used to be, especially when she showed up and the guy really did come up with a grand, once they got a look at her, hours ago.

He crosses the room and answers the door. Sera walks past him, sitting down primly at the foot of the bed.

"They tipped me another hundred," she says. "They wanted my number, but I told them to talk to you." She looks over at the television and seems a little disappointed to find it turned off. "Do you want it, the hundred I mean?"

Arms folded, he looms over her. Neither one of them realize that he looks only as threatening as an unhealthy man can look.

"How was the trick?" he asks, and with the question comes the realization, to him at least, that he is way out of practice.

Oddly, it is Sera who reflexively falls into a groove. The chat having always been part of the gig, she again has someone to chat to, and her speech flows more freely than it has since Al first made himself known to her. "Could have been worse," she says. "They use a lot of gimmicks, some big stuff… I'm a little sore. Reminded me of those two dykes in Brentwood." Looking up at him: "Remember? They always wanted me and Wendy." She continues on his belated nod. "He of course spent half the time watching from the corner of the room. You should see how they are. They love themselves for doing this." She looks down at the shag carpet, carefully. "You get her? I mean, did you pick up on her? She's a junkie… made me watch her shoot up."

Al doesn't know how to respond to this, for he missed this observation, and he shouldn't have. "You will need to work on the Strip tomorrow night. I have business all day. You like it best on the street. This will make you happy."

The flow gone from her words, Sera nods and says, "Could I keep it, the hundred I mean? You know I'm always straight with you, Al."

"Ah! It is a gift from Al," he says with a benevolent grin. "It is yours. Buy yourself a present from Al." He bows his head briefly—an old gesture she had forgotten—and begins to undress. "Now go shower for me, Sera. I have missed you tonight."

She blinks, and walks with difficulty to the bathroom. But inexplicably, it is the throbbing cut on her cheek that is the greatest source of her pain by the time she reaches the sinks.

The bathroom door shut, Al turns his attention to the mirror and manipulates his hair, here and around, with an unbreakable Ace comb. On the dresser, reflected in the mirror-world, he reads the alphabetical mess on a confused promotional pamphlet: ƎHT ⱯЯAHAƧ HOTEL INVITES YOU TO DISCOVER THE GOOD LIFE. He hears the shower start up. He considers his jewelry: he should go and get it tomorrow.

Eventually returning to his bed, this time naked, Sera finds that her indifference has grown, her diffidence flagged, her acceptance become all-consuming, like a well-matured cancer.

She takes him into her as if he were a trick; perhaps the biggest, baddest, god-trick of all time, but still a trick. He rocks on her, wrapped tightly in his own thoughts. She is a hollow doll, a million billion miles away from an orgasm. Al's a vigorous lover, and she knows that this will go on for a long time; in fact, this all could go on forever.

She anticipated some pain, but now she finds that she can barely feel him. His penis, though quite large, is causing merely an imprecise pressure inside of her, like the willful abuse of a post-Novocain dentist's drill. It's new to her, this numbness. In all these years she's always *felt* it, and she vaguely pines for the pain that summarized her dignity. He can't hurt her now. He can—and will—do whatever he wants to her, but he can't hurt her. Anyone can do anything to her; she couldn't care less.

♣  ♣  ♣

And now, the sun. Just the top of an orange disk visible through his open window, it always moves with unexpected swiftness at rise and set. Al has been waiting, watching for hours in the darkness of his room, and the Strip is remarkably silent and still.

He told Sera to leave at some time during the night—he can't remember when—and came to this window, sat down and crossed his legs. His erection is still with him, looking out of place as men's erections do and causing him great distress, throbbing and aching relentlessly. At first he was quite proud, pounding into her with no end in sight; he imagined her to be frightened, delighted, impressed. Then an hour passed, and he still was not delivered. In pain himself, he dare not even think of how she was holding up, and it was pure determination and fear of humiliation that drove him well into the next hour, when finally he rolled off of her and sent her away. He feels no excitement, no concupiscence, yet still his penis burns hard, threatening to split his skin. Afraid even to touch it, he tries to concentrate on the sun as a way to distract his misery.

Years ago Gamal Fathi, a boy in Oman when that country was all but sealed off from the twentieth century by Sultan Said ibn Taimur, had a sister named Manal who fell ill with a mysterious sickness that drove her to her mattress with fever and shivers. After four days his father, a man of some limited wealth, went in search of medicine to the home of an aging European who was rumored to have such things. The quest, dangerous, very expensive, and of dubious legality, was successful to the degree that he returned with a clay pot of prescribed liquid before it was too late. Everyone had considered the journey to be impossible and rejoiced at the miraculous accomplishment, convinced that the will of Allah had been revealed to them. And because of this, their grief was that much more unbearable when, after drinking the medicine, Manal convulsed and died within the hour. Gamal felt tricked, his young mind unable to follow the logic of the purpose. His father set off to kill the man who sold him the medicine, and he never returned.

Al's erection has at last died. A knock at his door startles him—odd for this hour of the morning. Pulling his pants on, he goes to answer it.

"Who is there?" he says, his hand on the knob, instinctively prepared to pull or push in an instant.

A young voice from the other side answers, "Service, Mr. Frisk. I have your breakfast. Shall I use my key?"

Disappointed by the apparent lack of intrigue, Al throws open the door with the intention of berating the boy for his mistake: "Why do you bother me!…," but is stopped by the sight of the face, wide-eyed and whitened with fear, purely American, and as such, both bland and limitless. "You have the wrong room," says

Al, in a much subdued tone, a virtual whisper.

The boy extracts a green piece of paper from his uniform pocket and looks at it. Unsteadily, he says, "Sorry, sir. I'm sorry." He looks at the number on the door. "Oh... oh no. I'm on the wrong floor. I'm so sorry to wake you, sir. I got off on the wrong floor." An attempted smile and a clumsy half-bow, and he is off on his way, the sound of a squeaky wheel on his cart Dopplering away to the hungry Mr. Frisk.

"I wasn't sleeping," says Al in an impossibly low voice. He knows the boy couldn't have heard him.

He goes into the bathroom, and after shutting tightly the door, lies down on the floor. He feels the cold hard tile against his ribs, porcelain at his back and colder still. It is not as it used to be. Something is wrong with Sera. She is soft; he is too easy, perhaps out of practice. Everyone stares at him, yet no one knows him— he knows no one. Las Vegas stinks. It is loud and hot. He hates this city, his little room.

plums

This will undoubtedly
days, thinks Ben as h
wrist, expecting to see

go on for the next few

e stares at his naked

but failing to find his

once prized Rolex. The watch has been swapped as planned for a few dollars at one of Las Vegas' always cheerful pawn shops. Now, instead of a thirty-five hundred dollar Swiss watch, Ben has two hundred and fifty dollars and a vacant wrist—a bargain to go along with his basement. Rather than blend this money in with his working capital, he decides to keep it apart and use it deliberately for one single thing. After all, he didn't pawn the watch for money. He pawned it to reaffirm his commitment to himself, to serve as an evidential footnote in his final chapter. So it is appropriate that any incidental money received from the transaction be used to complete the composition, to create a symmetry of action. More than appropriate, it is important. It is important because he needs to have something be important.

Maybe an overpriced hooker would be a good choice, someone to accept his last blast of semen, his final genetic statement. Too well paid to douche in his hotel room, the girl would leave with soggy underpants and shower at home. Hours later, the last of his DNA—possibly surviving him—would be wiped off the back seat of a cab with a paper towel.

His room is actually more of a motel room than a hotel room, probably because it is part of a motel, not a hotel. He had planned to stay in one of the many colorful towers that decorate the Strip, but was unable to come to terms with the corporate mentality regarding a reasonable extended stay rate. There were other problems too. Slightly suspicious of his motives and doubtful about his condition, the big hotels he tried were reluctant to suspend maid service on a daily basis, and Ben didn't want a good bedridden binge interrupted by Mrs. Clean; he also didn't want anyone fucking with his liquor. He was ultimately able to negotiate acceptable terms with the manager/owner of the Whole Year Inn—read the Hole You're In—one of the smaller motels that stand on what could easily be imagined as vacant lots, up and down the Strip. For one hundred and fifty dollars Ben gets a room for a week, self-service at the maid's cornucopian cart, and unlimited use of the ice machine and pool—No Life Guard on Duty. If there's a problem he can always move to a hotel, though he is charged in advance for each week here. In any case, he'll try to time it so that he gets a good view for his last days on the Strip, and week in or week out, Bank of America will write *their* whole loss off.

Moving may take a few trips. Whenever he returns to his room he brings with him a bottle or two of something or other, and after less than a week here he already has quite a little stockpile of booze, a trick that he could never or would never manage in LA. Always have access to a drink. The little room holds several inventories. There are bottles under the bed, in the drawers of the particleboard dresser, on the toilet tank, one in the toilet tank, in his suitcase, small ones in the pockets of dirty clothes, chilled ones in a styrofoam cooler that he bought, and a few more under the bed—in case of an emergency. As he watches television and sucks vodka he can feel the presence of all his liquor, surrounding and always beckoning, comforting but not reassuring.

After pawning the watch this morning he spent some time at poolside, watching a fat family from the midwest splash around in the dirty water. They are staying at the motel for two days as part of their vacation and seem to be satisfied with the accommodations. Talking with them, Ben felt a great sense of admiration for their general contentment, but he knows that this wouldn't stand up to scrutiny; their life could no more work for him than his for them, nor would he want it to. He was also impressed with the friendliness that this cholesterol-ridden, white-skinned little family exuded, a virtue that tends to run rampant in the midwest. Now, after his swim, he takes it easy on his bed, in front of the television, putting the final touches on his argument to himself in favor of buying a girl tonight, and selling his car tomorrow.

The trip from Los Angeles, the last time that he has driven, was indeed difficult for him. At this late date it has become nearly impossible to strike the balance of maintenance in his blood alcohol level. The line between too much and too little has long since become far too fine for his blurred vision to discern. So he is loath to get behind the wheel and jeopardize his best laid plans, not to mention the well being of the population of Las Vegas. There are cabs available anywhere, anytime in this city should he feel the urge to go someplace far. Las Vegas has also helped to rejuvenate his penchant for walking. Though he is physically no longer capable of the long, brisk walks that he used to take around Venice, he is perfectly happy to stumble up and down the Strip at night, swerving and tripping, a menace only to himself. Vegas has always had this attraction for him, the world's most amusing walking grounds, sober or drunk. So really his car has become something of a liability, a loose end. He can imagine it now: he's lying on the bed, sighing with relief as he realizes that he is gasping for his last breath, only to be interrupted—saved—by the manager/owner of the Whole Year Inn, who has come by to complain about the abandoned car in his parking lot. More realistically, owning a car is not exactly conducive to the anonymity that he is seeking here. The car must go. Tomorrow he will take it to one of the resale lots on Fremont and no doubt strike as good of a bargain for it as he did for the Rolex this morning.

As far as a hooker goes, concerning the skirt, pussy to be bought and paid for, perhaps even actually indulged in, his feeling is: of course. He wants to talk to a girl, a girl, girl, girl, girl. If his dick still works maybe he will even fuck her. His money is holding out just fine and can be easily concealed. He no longer has anything else to lose. At this point in his life—very nearly the period—the only thing that he could possibly crave, the only non-alcoholic thing, is a warm body. Up close evidence that life does go on. This will be his secret bargain, his revenge many times over for the watch and the car. He'll pilfer this little piece of ecstasy from a girl who thinks that he is paying for mere sex. She'll come to him, wielding her savvy and thrusting forth her hard earned survival, and he, unbeknownst to her, will suck off an extra hour for his own life. He will feel her heart beat and sit in joyous wonder of her, someone who takes the trouble to work so hard just to live so hard: a neat trick.

♣    ♣    ♣

Sera, looking rather glum and spectral, yet more intact than she has recently, stands on the sidewalk with her hands on her hips. The bruises that adorned her face have run away during the night, much the same way that they appeared, leaving only the cut on her cheek to suckle nutrition as it matures into Al's indelible signature. Moving headlights catch and play with her features, little shadows dance lightly over her impassive eyes. Pursuant to Al's request, she is working the Strip tonight. But something is missing, and she can't imagine how she once took such satisfaction in standing on this little patch of sidewalk... This little patch of sidewalk... Not unlike a confused cat on a dark road, she is experiencing one of those dormant moments of self-hypnosis and is somewhat mesmerized by the traffic. The slam of a car door stirs her, and she turns toward the sound.

Ben is standing on the driver's side of his car. "Hello," he says.

"Hello. You shouldn't stand out on the street like that. You might get hit," says Sera.

"Are you working?" he asks.

"Working? What do you mean working? I'm walking," she says.

As if to demonstrate walking she takes a few steps and pauses on the passenger side of the car. They look at each other across the roof. Ben is quite taken with this girl, with her dark beauty, and so remains silent rather than say the wrong thing. Far from the mechanical process of picking up a prostitute, to him this is more like asking for a date. He looks around. If he waits too long she will be suspicious and leave. If he is anything but direct she will think he's a cop. He reaches into the car and grabs the can of beer that he was drinking before he stopped. After draining it quickly, he tosses it back into the car.

"Isn't it illegal to drink and drive?" she says.

"That's funny," he says. "I wonder if you'll take two hundred and fifty dollars to fuck me? That is, if you'll come to my room for an hour I'll give you two hundred and fifty dollars."

He bites his lip and waits for her response. His never-steady nerves are not helped by the modified moderation that he attempted this evening in anticipation of driving. Less than a mile away, his roomful of liquor beckons.

"You're pretty drunk," she says.

Seeing that she will go with him, he relaxes a little and says, "Not really. My room's not far—the Whole Year Inn—you can drive if you want, or we can walk, or I'll give you cab fare, whatever you want. I'm in room number two."

"Why don't you give me the money when we get in the car, and I'll drive with you," she says, her hand now on the door handle. She falls easily into the groove of another trick, another simple hour of doing what she's told and getting some more bread for Al. It allays her anxiety, this procedure; it has too quickly become her only sure way to draw approval from him, the cheese at the center of her rat's maze.

Ben gets behind the wheel and reaches over to unlock the passenger door.

"I'm Ben," he says as he hands her the money, freshly extracted from his left front pocket.

"Hi. I'm Sera." And as if momentarily beheld by a doppelganger, she hears herself say, "That's with an E, S-E-R-A, Sera."

They shake hands then smile together at this. Though her smile seems to be in reaction to his, she is pleased to have impulsively identified herself to him in a way that was slightly beyond the call of duty. It felt clean, like the first totally self-motivated thing she has done in days.

Ben pulls back out into traffic for the short drive ahead. Instantly there is between them, however slight, that elusive chemistry which occurs only occasionally when two people meet. Always a welcome surprise, it is a sort of quick familiarity, implied permission to conduct relations at a level which is a bit deeper than the superficiality of introduction. Ben senses this and is beaming. But realistically he knows that his alcohol riddled brain may be overstating the case and that an hour from now he will never see this girl again. Though she is much friendlier than other hookers he has met and seems to like him, she is with him because he gave her two hundred and fifty dollars. She would probably be here whether she liked him or not, regardless of how much liquor per day he may be consuming, irrespective of any need she might perceive in him. And then it hits him. He adores this girl because she has a valid reason for liking him: two hundred and fifty dollars.

"I'm sort of curious," she says as they near the motel. "If you're willing to pay me two fifty—not that I mind... I mean, I'm okay with that—why aren't you staying at a real hotel? I have the feeling that you can afford it."

"We can go to one if you like," he says quickly, worried over her disapproval.

"No, this is fine. I was just wondering," she says.

He pulls into the parking space in front of his room, tires spanning the white spray painted 2 on the blacktop. "Well," he says, turning to her, "I'm here because I'm a drunk who tends to pass out at odd hours for unpredictable stretches. They're willing to leave me alone here as long as I pay for the room by the week, in advance. But it is sort of dreary. I'll probably move to a hotel soon, a room with a balcony for me to pass out on... or off."

Turning off the car he falls silent but makes no motion to open the door. Sera waits for something to happen. Common wisdom would indicate that she should be a little apprehensive but her instincts tell her differently; this person wishes her no harm. Too, she hasn't felt inclined toward apprehension lately. She has quickly faded into an observational fatalism—or is it bland apathy? She doesn't really care. She knows only that Al has certain expectations of her.

"Umm," she starts, trying to break the silence gently, "we can stay here in the car for an hour if you want, but I really have to go then. It's your time."

"Right," he says. "Sorry. I tend to fade in and out lately." Finding this quirk genuinely amusing, he smiles. "I'll get your door."

"I guess I do too," she says, almost to herself.

"You what?" He didn't quite hear her, but he wants to encourage even this, assuming it to be her patter.

"I sometimes fade out." A little embarrassed, irritated at the repetition, she would have denied having spoken at all but failed to think quickly enough.

He is caught off guard, surprised by her candor. "Oh... well, maybe we'd better synchronize our spells... or stagger them," and he half grins, half frowns, ready to support her reaction to his quip.

"You were going to get my door."

He rises out of the car and crosses over to her side, pleasantly surprised to see that she is indeed waiting for him to open her door. His arm offered and accepted, they leave the car and proceed to the room. The orange Day-Glo door opens with a tiny click, and Ben pats the wall immediately to his right, searching for the light. The switch is flicked and the room springs to life, telling its story to Sera.

"What this place needs," she says sarcastically, looking here and there at all the stashed bottles, "is a few more bottles of booze stashed here and there."

"Probably," he says.

Standing five foot four to his six feet, and at arm's length, she looks up at him and says with a tentative frown, "Why don't you undress. Mind if I use the bathroom?"

"Of course. Want a drink? I'm having one."

"A shot of tequila, if you can spare it, and a beer," she says, her tone laced with undirected defiance, and closes the bathroom door.

Ben feels like a teenager on his first date. A shot, a beer, and sarcasm to boot: this girl may be perfect. After preparing her shot in a plastic motel cup and putting it, with a can of beer, on the nightstand, he impulsively downs as much bourbon as he can in one continuous swill—about six ounces—and puts the bottle down so that he can pick it up as if for the first time when she walks back into the room. The reflexive old habit surprises him, for he has not felt the need of this sort of sly drinking behavior since his wife left him. Hearing that the water is still running in the bathroom, rather than being watched in the awkward act of pulling off his pants, and in line with her suggestion, he quickly undresses and slides between the sheets.

Sera emerges from the bathroom wearing nothing except one of the Whole Year Inn towels wrapped around herself. But upon seeing that Ben is already undressed and in the bed, she nonchalantly discards the towel and walks naked to the nightstand where her drink is. Draining the cup with one swallow she sits on the bed next to him and pulls the sheet from over him.

She tells him prosaically, "For two fifty we can do pretty much anything you want. You've been drinking, so it might be better if I got on top, but the other way's fine too. I have some jelly in case you want to fuck my ass… that's up to you. If you want to come on my face that's okay too, just try to keep it out of my hair and eyes." She thinks about asking him not to hit her, but decides that he's not the kind that would anyway. In any case, he wears no rings, and it is doubtful that her cut would open from just a slap. "It stings my eyes, and I just washed my hair. I'll suck you for a while… to get started."

Before he can speak, he is in her mouth. Though he is hard, he knows he won't come: the experienced alcoholic whoremonger. Thinking that she will be more comfortable having done something, he lets her go on for a few minutes, but he wants a drink more than he wants a blowjob. He sits up, putting a hand on her shoulder as he does, and so indicates that he would like her to stop.

"Do you want to fuck now?" she asks.

"Maybe another drink first. More tequila?"

"Okay," she says. Then with piqued confusion, "Whatever. What's the story? Are you too drunk to come?"

Ben, just now refueled by the recently consumed bourbon, responds to her challenge. There is just enough liquor in his voice now to mask the tones of adolescent puppy love.

"I don't care about that," he says. "Just stay with me for a while. There's time left. You can have more money. You can drink all you want. You can even have my car; I'm selling it in the morning anyway. You can talk or listen. Just stay. That's what I want."

She sees that this is all true, and part of the hooker in her runs away from that vision. Nor does she have the tools to manage him; Al has taken them away. The vacuum remaining can be filled only by some of what is left of her real self. Befuddled, she drops her head in thought. She sees her breasts, her vagina. She could talk to him, she thinks. It might be nice to talk a little.

So, left with no good rap, and also because she wants to know, she asks, "Why are you selling your car?"

Having won he smiles and hands her drink to her. Propped up on his pillow with a girl and a bottle is exactly where he wanted to be, and that's where he is right now.

♣  ♣  ♣

A combination of discretion—he does not want her to think that he has time for such nonsense—and boredom—the girl seems to have a proclivity for mysterious disappearances—caused Al to make his last passes of the Strip and Sera's house relatively early in the night. He will see her in the morning.

And it will have to be a good performance, for once again he has been unable to make any contacts. Even strangers are avoiding him. In truth, Al himself is beginning to detect the odor of desperation; it seems to follow him around.

This morning, after being awake all night, he resolutely showered and dressed so that he might at last go and retrieve his pawned jewelry, only to end up at a slot machine trading silver dollars back and forth until, not-so-much to his surprise, it was dark outside, and he had lost more than two hundred dollars.

She'd better bring home a lot, he thinks, angrily stuffing another twenty in the patient garter before him. He contemptuously regards the men around him: all drunk and lecherous, not a shred of dignity to be found in the whole place. The women— he once owned many women that make these look like dogs—are prideless puppets. Without meaning or direction they stand naked before these pig-men, all for a few lousy pennies. "Another drink!" he yells, thrusting his glass in the air then slamming it back down on the table. She'd better bring home a lot, he thinks, lifting another twenty from his stack. The dancer gyrates down to accept it and spreads her legs for him. Al looks at her cunt, his eyes baleful and glassed over.

♣　♣　♣

Noticing through her kitchen window that the first light of morning is beginning to drive away the dark, Sera sits and continues to drink from the bottle of tequila that she pilfered from her trick last night. She had stayed and talked with him for over two hours, and would have stayed longer if he hadn't passed out. The tequila was taken as an improvised overtime payment, and because she wanted to go straight home without stopping to buy a bottle.

　　She is confused and intrigued by this man, Ben. He asked her none of the usual *What's it like...* or *Why do you...* or *How can you...* questions that she has always heard from well-meaning tricks in the past who have tried to be her buddypal. Many times she has been through the would-be-social-researcher scene that tends to pop up now and then with tricks who don't realize that they just want to fuck her or, worse, think that they want to save her. She has encountered all types of men with as many different quirks who, for one reason or another, must separate themselves from what they are doing and make it clear that they are her social and moral superiors. Ben showed no trace of this. The fact that he had paid her to suck his dick and to do whatever would have come next had no bearing on the conversation that followed, conversation which flowed from her so effortlessly that it might have occurred two weeks ago, when simple eloquence was still reflexive in her. Apart from a little superficial vanity, she can remember nothing deceptive about him, no pretense. He was drunk. He was gentle. He managed to speak to a part of her that had been hidden even from herself. If he would have acknowledged her as a whore—which he didn't—she is sure it would have been with the same matter-of-fact acceptance that he used when calling himself a drunk. He seems to have no use for judgments, not even of himself—if true, a vacuum that must make it difficult for him to get along—and she wonders if that is because he is him or because he is a drunk. In any case, it is refreshingly simple, a splash of spring water to rinse off some of the toxic waste she lives in.

He told her about his trip to Las Vegas, from the decision to get rid of all his stuff to the perilous drunken drive. They sat naked in the bed together, and she, still sore from Al's relentless pounding the night before, was glad for the break. Not wishing to appear overly interested in a trick, she failed to ask a lot of questions that she might have under different circumstances or that have occurred to her since. For instance, she isn't clear on why he came to town. He claims that he likes to drink around the clock, and while she can certainly believe that, she doesn't see where it can end; he didn't strike her as being a member of the privileged class. He also said that he likes anonymity and that Las Vegas is a good place to find it. Two weeks ago she would have agreed. But he doesn't seem to want to do anything but drink, and though that may be one more thing than what she wants, she can't reconcile him with her image of a drunk.

She let him talk, listening half out of interest and half out of acquiescence, and let the time limit pass because she was comfortable and he wasn't beating or pounding or pissing on her. His speech thickened gradually and then fell away. Thinking that he was in the middle of a pensive moment, she turned to look at him and was met by the sight of his rising and falling head snoring silently through an open mouth. After watching him for a few minutes she got dressed and called a cab, taking the bottle on her way out.

Now the morning is almost in full swing and she's ready for

bed. She pushes the bottle to the corner of her kitchen table, next to the money that Ben paid her, and goes into her bedroom. Dropping her robe on the floor, pushing him from her thoughts, she closes her eyes and waits for a dream.

♣  ♣  ♣

"Not even five hundred? I give you a full night on the street and this is the best you can do?" Al, unaccustomed to drink and feeling not at all well after last night's overindulgence in the watered-down alcohol of the strip club, stands barking in her face.

Awakened by his knock and still in her robe, Sera says, "I'm sorry, Al. It was a slow night. I…"—frantically trying to assemble her thoughts—"I just couldn't score."

"What do you think you are, a sixteen year old girl holding out on me in Hollywood? You know better than this, Sera." He slaps her, hard and quick with an open hand, a non-destructive, disciplinary slap.

And she likes it. She doesn't know why, but it tastes like the key to something, and she likes it. She tries for more. "Don't be ridiculous, Al. You know better than that. Maybe it's just that nobody wants to fuck a chick with a cut across her cheek. That's a new one for you, isn't it, Al? Damaging the merchandise? It's gonna scar, you know." She thrusts her cheek to him in bold illustration. Drunk with the liberty of masochism, she is amazed at her audacity. "Best stick to the old knife game, huh? Out of sight, out of mind?" She turns and grabs a steak knife from out of a drawer. Throwing it at his feet along with her robe, she shows him her backside. "Here! Go ahead, Al!" she says.

Motionless, he is in virtual shock at this vituperation. He looks down at the row of marks that runs across her buttock and down the back of her thigh. For all these years he has carried the same marks in his memory. *Don't worry, Sera,* he used to say, *Never on the face. Now just turn over for me.* So many tears. He gave her that gift. She is the only person to have ever witnessed his tears. That memory, this vision, her anger: it's all too much for him. "Where were you last night," he says, eyes wide and wild. His voice is shaking, under pressure as if he were about to explode.

"I told you. It was a bad night. I went to the Trop for a few drinks," she says, meeting his stare. She feels like a third person in the room, watching all this with only mild interest. *And now he kills me, now I sleep, and he will be gone.* But she also remembers the tears, and how each cut into her was really a much deeper cut into him. Hers, she knew even as she bled, would ultimately heal.

Part of him wants to squeeze the life from her with his hands, or beat her until her heart just quits. He has never killed a man, much less a woman. Maybe that is what is wrong with his life. Instead he retches, nauseated and vulnerable, and has to catch himself on the table to avoid falling to the floor.

Unbelievably, she wants to go to him, to help him. Nothing changes. She wants to absorb his pain.

Regaining what he can of himself, he stands. He has never seen this woman before. He will never enter this place again. He spits and says, "Work tonight. Bring me the money when you are done... no matter what the hour is." He turns and is gone, noise from the slammed door rattling after him.

"I will," she says, naked in the kitchen.

♣　♣　♣

Sera knows, although she hasn't yet realized, that she would like to see Ben—she thinks of him as *that drunk trick*—again. Her life has become somewhat pointless, and even passed out, he was still better company than anyone else she knows: an extremely exclusive club. Something about him—intimacy with black required to fully understand white—recalls for her the unique beauty of waking and working and eating and sleeping. Where is all of that now? Perhaps she felt it in his room.

So she is not at all surprised to find herself working the same stretch of sidewalk that she did last night when he picked her up. Every car that slows for her brings a fleeting moment of anticipation, which dies when she fails to recognize either car or driver. More argumentative than usual while negotiating price, she has lost a few customers and not really regretted it, preferring to stick around the street rather than take a chance of missing him or perhaps losing him to another girl for the night. For all she knows, he was so drunk that he doesn't even remember what she looks like, though she doubts that this is so. A white limousine pulls to the curb alongside of her, disrupting her thoughts, and she anticipates the forthcoming offer; it may be difficult to refuse.

In truth, she doesn't have any conscious ideas about what she might expect from Ben. Maybe he'll ask me to go steady, she thinks cynically, as a hot spray of semen hits the back of her throat. She is kneeling at the foot of a bed in a hotel suite, fulfilling her bargain with a Japanese businessman from Texas who offered her so much bread for a single blowjob that she couldn't say no. Spitting come into a hotel towel and pushing her hair back, she tells him that she has to leave and hurries back to the street, where she finds Ben seated at a bus stop and drinking out of a glass, as if he were at a cocktail party.

"Don't run away!" he says, holding out his palm reassuringly as he rises.

"Why should I?" she asks. Now that he is standing in front of her, and the situation she has constructed abstractly all night has become real, she is defensive and unsure. "I know you're not a

[ 136 ]

cop, so what is it tonight? Another two fifty to watch you sleep?"

"No," he sits back down, a little put off. "I couldn't remember what happened last night. I was afraid that I might have been mean or rude to you. If I was, I'm sorry."

"No, just drunk," she says, warming, "but that's okay."

"I came here hoping that I could find you again tonight. I can pay you if you want, but I'd rather just take you out as a friend. That is, I like you and would like to see you on a social basis, if you know what I mean. I don't know if you have a boyfriend, or for that matter, a girlfriend, but if you have some free time... maybe we could... have dinner."

"Are you serious?" she says, knowing that he is.

"If I'm at all clear about this—and we both know that I may not be—I think that you know I'm serious."

"When?" she asks.

"It's still early tonight, as if that matters in Las Vegas," he says, standing again, a little giddy now.

"I just turned a rich trick." This is spoken as a test, and she looks sharply at him for a reaction but fails to get one. "I can quit for the night. If you want to get something to eat, that's fine—you look like you could use it—but first I have to go home and shower. It won't take long, if you don't mind waiting. Where's your car?"

"I sold it this morning."

"I should have taken it when you offered." She is a little surprised to hear that he really meant to sell it, and this small revelation somehow adds validity to the rest of what he has said. "I bet you got a great price at one of our non-profit car dealers here in town."

"Just about enough to pay my cab fare back to the room. I don't care. I'm always too drunk to drive anymore. We'll take a cab to your place. It's my new hobby, taking cabs."

They both smile. Caught in the acceleration of a brand new

rapport, they share the unspoken anticipation of conversations yet to be had, society yet to be felt; they freshen with the recovery of long dormant skills which seem to be no less effective for their lack of practice. Oddly, it is Sera, between the two of them, who embraces most readily the spark, still just a speck in her peripheral vision. Her inner voice speaks to her of thirst and memory.

"We should stop for a bottle of tequila," she says. "I owe you a bottle of tequila.

"You certainly do," he says.

After crossing the street and picking up the liquor, which she insists on paying for, they flag down one of the readily available Las Vegas taxicabs and start the short ride to her apartment. She has never allowed a trick to see where she lives, not that any of them would have necessarily cared to; Sera was not the regular customer type. But then, Ben lost his customer status at the very moment that she decided to take him to her home.

♣　♣　♣

Home in his sweetroom, as home as it gets anyway, Al can hear voices emanating from the other side of the wall behind his headboard, the room next to his. Completely absorbed, he has been sitting in the dark for hours, trying to follow the thread of conversation between these strangers.

"...six hours... believe... every time... couldn't sit still... nursery school..."

At the foot of his bed is an overturned room service tray. Potatoes and lamb, still uncut, litter the floor, peas and raisins sail on a puddle of tea, steeped to an indeterminate degree. Al has no recollection of how this happened, for when he awakened from an earlier nap to the sound of these voices, the mess had already been made. It was to be his dinner.

"...fix it for... paycheck... open at... lifeguard..."

Al listens, eyes very wide. He could have sworn they said his name not one hour ago. Perhaps he has been too obvious here in Las Vegas, asking around too much. He must learn to keep a lower profile. From now on he must be very careful.

♣  ♣  ♣

"You know, I saw you last week," she says, taking another exploratory step. "I saw you fall down on the sidewalk."

"No kidding? Which time? Last week I fell down two times—two that I know about. Hang around with me and you'll get to see it a lot," he says.

Choosing not yet to address the pros and cons of falling down habitually, she says, "It was not far from where you're staying, but on the other side of the street, and late at night, early in the week. I shouted to you, but I don't think you heard me. You fell down and didn't move, and I was afraid that you might attract the cops—you know, lying there looking like a corpse." This last is meant to be humorous, but she instantly regrets it, realizing for the first time that he does, in some ways, look a little too sick.

"I didn't think I was down that long. Didn't I just get right up and walk away?"

"Well, I don't know. I guess. You say you're used to it, but seeing you fall like that had me worried." Her pronunciation of *worried* is accompanied by a raised eyebrow and a look that cuts right to him. This hint of affection stymies the prattle, and fearing that she may have gone too far, she backs off. "I worry about everybody," she says.

"I know that you do," he says. The cab pulls to the curb in front of her apartment building. They are at her home.

With Sera in the shower and Ben a first time visitor, the

apartment itself becomes a passive participant in their evening. Conspicuous in its silence, much like a sequestered house cat, it watches Ben with a dubious eye. He sits patiently waiting at the kitchen table where Sera left him. Then rising with polite curiosity, he shuffles around the room, one hand holding a glass and the other pausing here and there to pick up and inspect various objects, first in the kitchen, and then boldly into her living room.

Her possessions are indeed few and far between, and what there is has been arranged with a great sense of order. He sees his past self in her neatness, and this revelation comforts him. There is in the kitchen a collection of fifteen or twenty souvenir toothpick holders. Most bearing enameled legends of this city: *I was PICKED KLEEN in LAS VEGAS, NEVADA*, they are each filled with an appropriate quantity of toothpicks, their respective capacities observed to the pick. Gifts to herself, intentionally tacky, he guesses, the product of a slow night on the Strip. His hands pass over them in reverence, for they are no doubt important to her. Taped to the refrigerator is a greeting card photograph of a kitten and a ball of yarn. Upon flipping it open to read the signature inside, he finds the card blank and dismisses its presence here on the fridge as part of a feminine affinity for this type of image. The furniture, neither expensive nor creative, is tasteful at best. The girl clearly has no aspirations in the field of interior design. In fact, he notices, this apartment sports a general paucity of art in any conventional form. Like a Shaker home, this place platonically denies all but function, and for that reason aspires to a higher level of art: a deliberate art of basic reality. The television is black and white and looks to be rarely used. There is a simple radio on a bookshelf, which also contains a respectable collection of English and American literature, all in paperback. The carpet is gray indoor/outdoor, the sofa linen; there are no shags or velours, no pinks or lime-greens. The apartment reflects no

preoccupation with high-end consumer electronics, no fascination with media, no periodicals, no posters, no paintings. Yet it
has none of the make-do atmosphere of poverty. Nor does it show
evidence of the haphazardry, the random guesses at quality, so
often found in the dwellings of the unimaginative. Ben spins on
his heel, watches the room blur, and stops too quickly at the sound
of the shower being turned off, sloshing part of his drink on to the
floor. This place offers no definitions of its occupant. This, he
decides, is the home of an angel.

"You okay out there?" Sera calls from the bathroom.

"Of course. Why, shouldn't I be? Take your time, I'm fine."
He goes back into the kitchen and pours himself another drink.

Her muffled voice continues, "I won't be long. Make yourself
another drink."

He sits waiting, drinking at the table. A few minutes later,
upon entering the room, Sera finds him staring at the floor,
motionless.

"You okay?" she says.

He seems not to hear and then responds, smiling at the
repetition, "Of course. You look beautiful."

"Thank you." But a concerned look visits her face, and she
finds herself even more aware of just how not-okay he
is. "It must be late," she says. "What time have you got."

"Sorry. My watch went the way of my car. I'm not only too
drunk to drive anymore, but I'm also too drunk to participate in
the world of timekeeping—even as an observer." He holds up his
empty wrist, his drink with the other hand. "Two hairs past a
freckle. See, in LA I kept running out of liquor after it was too late
to go out and buy some. For some reason the clear-cut solution
was to move someplace where it is never too late. And, of course,
now that I'm here I seem to have solved my stocking problem—
you saw my room. But that sort of backward up-sweeping comes

[ 141 ]

as no surprise. Anyway, I was getting tired of being looked at funny when I would walk into a bar at six a.m.. Even the bartenders in my neighborhood started preaching to me. Here people drink at all hours. No one cares. There may be legitimate reasons, vacations and whatnot, but it just doesn't matter because they're not from here. They're not overtly fucking up." He pauses, afraid that too much is being said too soon. "I'm rambling. I really like you. You make me want to talk. I don't know what time it is."

"I like hearing you talk," she says, and means it. "If you feel up to a short walk we can go to a place just up on the corner. All the food in Las Vegas is terrible anyhow, and this way we won't have to wait for a cab. How does that sound to you?"

"Drinks?" asks Ben, but he really doesn't care. He can carry his own if necessary. They go off on their way down the street, walking. That sounded just fine to him.

Talking effortlessly at the restaurant, they continue to pursue the tangential conversations that go with new acquaintance. This acquaintance, however, is maturing faster than most. Both of them feel an unspoken urgency to their friendship. Beyond the more obvious time factor that Ben feels, this impatience is due to an even more immediate need that they share. A vacuum, long unaddressed in Sera and always fundamental in Ben, is being looked at and considered. They are recognizing an opportunity to prevent an emotional tragedy. They are struggling with the bewilderment of finding that a long-held assumption may not be so. They are, at once, seeing for the first time decisions that they may have made and unexpected options that they may now have.

To Ben these feelings are apart from what he is doing to himself. The short term that he has assigned to his own life is having its effect on his mentality beyond his day to day conduct change. He believes that dying, dying soon, is an unalterable fact of his life, and as it becomes more deeply rooted in his reality, he thinks of it no more than anyone else thinks of their own natural death; he is aware of it, but not obsessed with it. Subtly, though, his actions have taken on added significance to him. The governors have all been removed and he now looks for the direct and deliberate, embracing the aggressive and shunning the abusive. With the specter of the finite looming very near, Ben can almost envisage this time as a microcosm of his whole life, a narrow but tall area, to be played very intensely. So a girl is a girlfriend, and a girlfriend is everything. It is the psychology of a fourteen year old, who is also disinterested in the not-so-foreseeable future. Ben adores Sera, would like her to be a part of his life. But changing his life, extending it, is no longer an option that would occur to him. She should accept that context in the same way that he has. Though it may be wishful, he sees in her the capacity to do this; it is what he considers to be her charm.

"So why are you a drunk?" asks Sera. She had been watching him pick over the small, undressed salad he ordered in lieu of dinner. He finally pushed it away and called for another drink.

"Is that what you want to ask me?" he says, measuring.

"Yes." She knows that this is more than a question and is willing to stand her ground.

"Well," he says, "then I guess this is our first date or our last. Until now, I wasn't sure it was either."

"Very clever. Fine. First. It's the first." She surrenders this. "I'm concerned. Why are you killing yourself?"

"Interesting choice of words," he says. Then, after a pause, he says almost to himself and as if out of frustration, "I don't remember. I just know that I want to."

"Want to what? Kill yourself? Are you saying that you're drinking as a way to kill yourself?" She leans over the table, close to him, listening intently.

"Or killing myself as a way to drink," he says and laughs playfully. He has decided not to deal with this apparently inevitable discussion yet. Maybe he'll die in the rest room and so avoid it. But in fact he is not sure just how silly his answer is. He is not at all sure about any of the how or why questions anymore. He no longer cares to address them.

Annoyed, she lets it go. But she too can see that this is unfinished business, though in a way it seems less than imperative, almost irrelevant, certainly not worth risking things right now. In all fairness she considers that she, herself, would not care tonight to expound the happy-go-lucky world of prostitution, and she is again impressed by his failure to bring that up. Sera tries not to look too deeply at things anymore, for fear that they may not hold up to scrutiny. Everything should roll along, and she should be able to just play her part. She likes being here, and it feels good to like something. So she can see no reason to fuck it all up by challenging this man, Ben, over his life plan.

Her own life plan these days is limited to just about that. Plan: stay alive. If she has to sell her soul to make that work, then fine. At least her blood doesn't flow as freely as it once did, and he sleeps somewhere else. Now some guy wants to come up her ass— okay. Maybe Al wants to start sticking her with the knife again— no problem. She's older now, more mature. Everything's different than before, when she was a kid and used to fret over such things. She can turn off now, let it happen and still wake up in the morning. And if the cut runs too deep and she doesn't wake up, well at least it won't be by her own hand; she will have played out her part. After all, there's really only one not-so-fine line. Everyone is so proud of their own insignificant little boundaries. Scrupulously they vow, *I would never do that!* And perhaps they wouldn't. More likely, they'll never have to. Anyway, that's them, that's fine. Not all men want to do that to her. Some men like her. A lot of guys appreciate her. She helps them out. It feels good to help people. It's a bonus to being alive. Icing on the cake. Everything's working out just fine.

"Ben," she says, watching him suck out of his glass, watching gin dribble down his puffy face. "Why don't you stay at my apartment tonight? I mean…," she falters, "Look, you're so drunk—or you will be soon, at this rate—you could sleep on my couch. I trust you. I like you. Don't make a big deal, but I hate to think of you at that cheesy motel. You seem so alone… I mean… Let's face it: What the fuck are you doing in Las Vegas?" And with this blurted out, she sits back to enjoy her resolve. Despite the amused look on his face, she is secure in her deployment of that ultimate authority that all women ought to have over all men. All real men.

"That's astonishing, Sera. Or maybe it isn't." He is pro-foundly moved by her offer, as he always is by any overt show of compassion. His initial surprise is mitigated as he realizes that this type of behavior is very much a part of her, that she is indeed good. "Don't worry. I told you, I'm going to move to a hotel soon—tomorrow, if it will make you feel better. Thank you, but I'm fine. I'll just pass out. Let's talk about tomorrow: wanna do something?" He likes the youthful sound of this simple question crossing his lips, but it is followed by a cough, and a gasp for breath.

"Sure. Let's do something tonight first. We have to take a cab to the Sahara so I can drop off something personal. Then please stay at my place. Do it for me. We can talk till late and sleep till late. As you know, I am my own boss."

At this he starts laughing. Sera, though startled by the unintentional irony of her remark, laughs to join him. In the mirth he assents. But his hesitation was genuine, for he is in love with her, and he must be careful—oh, so careful.

♣   ♣   ♣

Not too early, not too late, the hour is about right for her to be here. She warned Ben, now waiting down at the main bar, that she might be a few minutes. Fortunately he is quite willing to be left at a bar and didn't act at all concerned. Nor was he curious about her errand, though this, she supposes, is out of polite regard for her earlier use of the word *personal*. She knocks on the door with surprising insistence, considering whose door it is, and it seems to buckle under her fist.

"Yes? What?" The muffled voice sounds strange to her: Al, but not Al.

"It's me, Al."

He opens the door, first just a crack, then fully. "Sera," he says, straightening his back and his face. "It's…" He looks around, presumably for a clock, but fails to find one. "It's late," he asserts, as if the absence of a clock is a sure sign of lateness.

She ducks past him into the room. "Sorry, Al. Good night, lots of tricks," she lies, digging from her purse the seven hundred odd dollars she has—most of it from the overpriced head—and handing it to him. "I think things are picking up."

He doesn't respond, just takes the money silently and puts his finger to his lips, apparently listening for something. She notices a film of sweat on him, and it worries her. She suddenly does not want to be alone with him. She feels weak in the knees.

Standing next to his bed, he looks at her and with one finger still on his lips beckons her with the other. His single ring dully reflecting a forty-watt nightstand light. *Where's all your jewelry, Al?*

Okay. She has no choice. Five minutes ago she thought about

this contingency when she hinted to Ben that her errand might drag on a bit longer than expected. Now she's amazed at how much she doesn't want to do this; suddenly she doesn't feel all that numb. Dropping her purse on the foot of the bed, she begins unbuttoning her blouse.

But he waves her off, shakes his head vigorously, and whispers, "Have you told anyone that I am here?"

Confused, frightened by his strange behavior, and maybe just a little miffed despite herself, she wants to say, *Who am I gonna tell, Al? Who the fuck's supposed to care?* but she says, "No." She stands, waiting, unsure of whether or not she should continue to undress, braced for his fury if she guesses wrong.

The sweat is pouring from him. He wants to ask her. He wants to tell her. He really, really wants to beg her to stay and listen with him, to tell him why these strangers in the room next to his are talking about him. It would be so easy: *Do you hear that?* But she wouldn't. She hates him, he knows, and she would pretend to hear nothing. He is completely alone. Now, of all times, he cannot afford to appear weak in her eyes. "Go, Sera," he whispers. Then, because he has to, again in a louder voice: "Go, Sera. Stay at home. I will call you tomorrow."

She stares at him with growing concern, a messy concern for both tormented and tormentor, an amalgamated concern for everyone who is fucked, whether they know it or not. He reminds her of the boy throwing up in the corner of the cheap motel room—a lifetime and some harmless bruises ago. She wants him to hit her, to be himself, but this time she wants it for him instead of for her. "Are y...," she starts, but is cut off with a frantic motion.

He turns to her and says patiently, in a low voice, "Sera, please go. This is very important to both of us. I am setting up a very big deal. This is about our trick, and I must listen."

*Hit me! Fuck me! Give me something familiar. Please!*
Unable to comprehend, her feet feel frozen, until he again waves
her away with a ridiculous, almost slapstick gesture, sweat flying
from his head as it shakes vigorously. She leaves his room,
unwittingly popping a button as she undoes her undressing.

♣   ♣   ♣

As things happen, with the occasional seemliness of fate, Sera's
one night invitation to Ben evolves into an unspoken arrangement between the two of them. Sera, thirsty beyond even her own
reckoning for companionship, has easily taken to his comfortable, accepting manner, his subtle, sincere devotion. By not
verbalizing any definite plan, she is able to maintain the confirmed independence of those who live alone, while satisfying the
craving for friendship which has gone mostly unanswered in her
and is now burning with heretofore unsuspected intensity.

Beyond these universal needs he is functioning as a catalyst of
her catharsis. He is a lever with which she is attempting to impel
Al from her soul, for she has learned that to run away is nothing
more than a quick fix. Ben, hours, days, and nights all blending
together for him, is willingly manipulated into the situation;
indeed, to him it is a most benign manipulation, and he is
inwardly grateful for being given a function to serve.

Sera has not called Al, now to her an unknown quantity,
volatile and strange. Nor did she respond two days ago to the
ringing of her phone, this an impulse which seized her as quickly
as the harsh ring had startled her; they had been sitting on the
floor, and Ben had just grabbed her knee as part of a punch line
delivery. There were only three rings, one series, nothing since,
and she finds this protracted silence terrifying, knowing as she

does that he will soon have to be dealt with. Perhaps even now he lurks, scorned and desperate, outside her window. Ignorant of the menace—she has kept Al a secret—Ben, who is often too drunk to walk, much less fight, still manages to passively impart to her a sort of vanilla intrepidity; or does he simply conjure it from where it sleeps within her?

For three days she and Ben have spent their time in one long, life-reviewing conversation, punctuated by excursions out for food, liquor, and a change of clothes for Ben. They have neither confessed their mutual infatuation nor continued the sexual relationship that might have been started in his motel room on the night of their first meeting. This afternoon, upon waking from a nap and finding him watching her from the corner of her bedroom, Sera chooses to consummate their cohabitation.

"Isn't your rent coming up at the motel?" she starts.

"Yeah, must be," he says. "I've sort of lost track of time here at Hotel Sera. I'll go take care of it today, or tonight, or whatever the next available solar segment is. Why don't you come with me and we'll find a real room for me? You can pick it out, a tower on the Strip."

"What I meant was that you should bring your stuff over here. What the fuck! We're spending all this time together as it is. There's no reason to blow all your money on a hotel room. Face it: we're having fun here. I think we can dispense with formality at this point. You know, Ben, if anything, I trust in your integrity completely. I want you here now. I'm not too concerned with long term plans, and as far as I can see, you don't seem to have any. Are we gonna screw around like kids? This is what I want. Why don't you go get your stuff?"

Ben wants her to be right, but he also knows that he's been drinking carefully, very measured, and she hasn't seen him at his worst; that can't go on. The closer he gets to her, the deeper he falls for her, the more he thinks that this might be a mistake. Maybe he was wrong. Maybe he shouldn't start anything with this girl. Things are set nicely for him to curl up and die as a stranger in Las Vegas, just like he planned. Why should he do it in this girl's lap. She shouldn't have to see that.

"Don't you think that you'll get a little bored living with a drunk?" he tries. "You haven't seen the worst of it yet. I knock things over. I throw up all the time. It's a miracle that I've felt so good these last few days. You're like some sort of antidote that mixes with the liquor and keeps me in balance, but that won't last forever. You'll get very tired of it very quickly." His eyes fix on a black dot, just a few feet from his corner. It is a spider, suspended on a single strand of either an old or future web, swaying with the currents of the room. This appears to be its only movement, so the spider may in fact be dead. He returns to her, mouth set defiantly: *wake up, sister.*

But she is determined. "Okay, so *then* you can move to a hotel, and I'll go back to my glamorous life of being alone. The only thing that I have to come home to now is a bottle of Listerine to wash the taste of come out of my mouth. I'm tired of being alone... that's what I'm tired of. Jesus Christ! Look at you! You look like you're about to drop dead. I want you here with me, and all you want to do is crawl off into a dark motel room. I can't face worrying about you. We gotta decide this right now, before we go any further. You either stay here with me, or I can't see you anymore." She wonders if she should tell him about Al. She's hoping to deal with him in his suite, and let it all become just a story to be told later, but part of her insistence with Ben might be motivated by plain fear; she owes him more.

The room is silent as he burns under her demanding gaze. He must respond, and he hates this kind of pressure. As the quiver starts in his neck, he picks up his shaking hand and empties the cup of vodka, which he has been nursing, down his throat.

"What you don't understand is...," he begins, wanting to come clean with her, to tell her not to worry about the cost of the room because it will all be handled by his plastic estate; in other words, to tell her that he not only wants to crawl off into a dark motel room, but that he really does want to die there as well. But it is too much, too unkind. This isn't what she wants to hear, and it certainly isn't what he wants to say. No, he's still alive and he wants to be with her. She apparently wants to be with him. So what's the problem? He'll spend some time here; then, when things get really bad, he'll move to a hotel. She'll probably be glad to get rid of him. He starts again. "You can never hassle me about drinking," he warns.

"I understand that," she says, nodding. "I really do understand that." Now she is smiling. "I want to do some shopping alone. You go out for a few drinks and then get your things. Don't hurry, and I'll be back before you to let you in. I'll have a key made while I'm out."

Having thus penetrated this barrier, Sera springs from the bed and pounces on him with an uncharacteristic exuberance, catching him in a fervent embrace that is fueled by years of untapped emotion. She herself is caught off guard by her passion, and the room darkens happily to her eyes as his face fills her vision. Her kisses flow unchecked, uncounted, unmeasured, from his cheek to his chin to his eyes and again; so many fast kisses, each one a veritable possession.

♣    ♣    ♣

Ben stands for the last time in the Whole Year Inn. Freshly showered and changed into his black suit—just out of the cleaner's plastic—and collarless white parson's shirt—slightly dirty, still smells okay—he is feeling pretty sharp, though walking a little unsteadily. Resolutions always ease his mind, and this one gets more pleasing to him the more he thinks about it. Sera's emotional outburst convinced him that he had said the right thing, made the right move.

Into his suitcase he is collecting the full and mostly full bottles of liquor that litter his room. The few nearly empty bottles that he finds—there are not many, he always tends to polish them off—he pours into a single cup, a sort of very Long Island iced tea. More like a Long Three-Mile Island iced tea, he thinks. Repeatedly he circles the room, until, with the bottles all packed— one in his jacket pocket—and the suitcase full, he remembers what he has forgotten and frowns at the heap of clothing and related items that he assembled on the bed. Already about as burdened with baggage as he intends to be, yet unwilling to leave his estate of so many personal threads to the administration of strangers, he is growing weary of the whole project. Then, recognizing a sterling opportunity, he takes all the plastic liners from the bottoms of the wastebaskets in the room and fills them with his clothes, all the things from LA, all the non-liquid things he has left to him. He ties off each bag, carries them all out to the trash bin at the rear of the motel, and dumps them out of his life. Returning to the room, he thinks how great this is. Now he has saved himself the embarrassment of physically moving in; he can simply *walk in* to her apartment. Also, she'll be saved the trouble of cleaning up a lot of junk should he ultimately not make it to a hotel. They'll have fun later shopping for a pair of jeans and a few shirts. Maybe he'll buy two dozen pairs of underwear and sox and never have to wash them again, just throw them out and wear new ones each day: one of the privileges of the ebbing class. Jamming his money deep inside his left front pocket, he calls a cab, drains his cup, and with some effort, lifts his suitcase and clinks happily out the door.

♣    ♣    ♣

"That's it then? You're happy?" asks the well made-up salesgirl. She looks to be about nineteen and contentedly caught in the web of cosmetic consumerism that Sera once capered in.

"Yes," says Sera. "That's all I need today. Could you possibly wrap them for me?"

"Gift wrap is on Two," says the girl. Smiling slyly, she is both intrigued by the romantic overtone and pleased to be passing the wrapping job upstairs.

Using a portion of the substantial savings withdrawal she made this morning—most of it intended to propitiate Al later—Sera pays for the two gifts and heads up the escalator. Unsure, at the time, of the moral implications, she had hesitated over the purchase of the silver flask, but it was only a very brief, momentary hesitation. Then, past the screen of media input and pop-logic, she picked out an ornate half-pint pocket flask. The sweet simplicity and well-evolved purity of this natural selection put her in an intellectual mood, enabled her maturity to size up the slick correctness of quick infatuation. Bang! Bang! The motivation is the message. She went to the loudest shirt rack in sight and picked out a bright pink and green jungle print. Big, puffy sleeved, baggy and conspicuous, she chose it to contrast with the black clothing that he seems so partial to. She chose it, as women will, to paint her name across his chest.

But for her it is a statement of support, not a notice of ownership. She savors her own delight in performing these commonplace acts, this gift shopping. With the shirt and the flask

[ 153 ]

on her arm, on their way to adornment in what will end up being a five dollar gift wrap, she rediscovers a side of her femininity that doesn't need to be cloaked in caution, doesn't require preliminary mistrust. She feels like a girlfriend.

Nothing like the way she feels as she stands outside of Al's door, almost four full days since her last *visit*. Like a warning beacon, the yellow Mercedes did not escape her notice downstairs. She purposefully had the cab cruise the back lot and was surprised to find that the car hadn't been moved since she last saw it. She takes a deep breath, purses her lips and blows out the air evenly, knocks gently on the door.

It is whisked open, catching her off guard and in a momentary vacuum. Al stands before her, fully dressed, his clothes looking as though they've been slept in more than once.

"I have waited. I have waited because I knew you would come," he says. Then, after taking a seat in one of the room's two white wicker chairs, he says, "Sera." This latter is spoken more as a statement than an address.

She watches him carefully and with a perverse reverence. His voice is absolutely void of any emotion whatsoever, and she has never heard anything quite like it. The room, saturated and lugubrious, is quiet for a long time.

"I brought you some money," she says, and it sounds trite and pathetic to her.

He looks at her with hollow eyes. He looks up from the chair at her. She is still standing, and when he looks at her he looks to her as if he were all scooped out.

"I must leave Las Vegas. You have come and now I can leave," he says. "But I have waited for you." A spark of desperation enters his tone. "Always remember that *I* have waited for *you*."

She notices that the matching wicker chair is burst through at the seat; unable to support his weight, she guesses. She prepares to speak, ready to deliver the speech she's been rehearsing all morning: *I can't come back here, Al. Not ever. I can't trick for you anymore. None of our past can ever happen again. Don't come to my house. Don't call me. I'll do whatever it takes. I'll go to the police. I'll incriminate myself... I don't care. Kill me now if you want, but when I leave this room, you can never touch me in any way again.*

Instead, she says, "Goodbye, Al. Go somewhere and try to get better. This is just history." She bends and kisses him on the forehead, tucks the money envelope into his lap, and leaves his room.

Ten minutes later Al himself leaves his room. A tip for the maid, his ring and gold chain lie cast-off and forgotten on the dresser.

But he has his clothes, and they are in the trunk of the Mercedes when it—mercifully—starts. He drives fast, but not too fast, skims by an indifferent state trooper, breezes by Henderson, the dam. 93, Kingman, no stops.

♣　♣　♣

"We didn't know whether to call the police or not," says her neighbor to Sera. Apparently waiting for her arrival, he has just stepped out of his door. Speaking cautiously, unsure of his sudden role in the life of this quiet, pretty girl who lives next to him, he indicates Ben's snoring body, curled up in front of Sera's door, clutching a pint of bourbon. "He's been there for about half an hour. My wife said she's seen you two together, so I decided to wait till you got home." Through his window he has watched Sera come home in the past, has always been aware of her proximity.

"Yes, thank you. He's my friend. I guess he just had a little too much to drink," says Sera, smiling uncomfortably. "I'll help him inside. Thanks for your concern, sorry to trouble you." She nods in conclusion and there is an awkward pause.

The man turns back to his door. "Well, call me if there's anything I can do," he says gallantly, for future reference.

She puts down her packages and opens her door, then kneels next to Ben. "Can you wake up?" she says, gently shaking him.

Opening his eyes, he looks at her and then around. "Hi," he says with a smile, as if they have just awakened from a Sunday afternoon nap.

She is taken in and finds her humor, which was never far anyway. "You're a very private guy, aren't you?" she says. Why don't you go in and sit down. I'll get this stuff. You have some gifts to open."

"Right. I figured," he says, rising. Halfway to erect he loses balance but catches himself on the doorjamb short of falling. "I'll go sit on the couch." Grabbing his suitcase, he manages to pull it after him and disappears into the house amidst the clink of the bottles. "Want a drink?" he calls. "Great nap. Wanna go out tonight?"

Sera, having never before closely witnessed the day to day endurance and rejuvenescence of a long-term drunk, is amazed, truly impressed. She's been expecting him to crash like this eventually, but she didn't think that it would only last for half an hour. She picks up her packages and enters the apartment, closing the door behind her.

"Seriously," she starts, finding him pouring two drinks in the kitchen. "I like to keep pretty low key around here. Maybe next time you could drop off inside the door."

"Oh, I always do. Don't worry. I'm sorry about that, but I got back too early and the door was locked."

"Of course," she says, thus falling into one of his oft used expressions as she reaches into her purse. "Gift number one." She holds out the duplicate door key to him.

Taking the key from her, he walks to the door and successfully turns the lock with it. "Pursuant to our conversation of this afternoon," he says, and drops the key into his pocket. "I used to carry a lot of keys, but one by one they fell victim to the great condensation. Now I have this one."

It seems as though he might continue, so she watches and listens. But soon it becomes apparent that he has lost his thought and is simply staring at the floor.

"Ben," she says, approaching him and placing her hand on his arm.

He looks up. "Sorry," he says, and brightens. He is returned. "More presents?" Turning, he picks up her glass and strides into the living room.

She looks after him thoughtfully, wondering at his energy, mustering her own. She'll be needing her newfound energy, all her many energies.

He is seated on the couch when she enters the room and puts the two packages on the table in front of him.

"I want you to let me pay your rent for this month. I'm here; I've come this far. It'll be better for me that way... okay?" he says, as if he cannot proceed any further until this is resolved.

"All right," she says. "Not that this has anything to do with that, but I plan to go out and do a little work—probably tomorrow night." She tries to sound resolute. Even though he has never made her feel uncomfortable about what she does, she is still unsure of what his reaction will be to this.

"Do you have an appointment?" he asks. Then, looking up quizzically, "You know, I've never really asked you much about your work. Do you have regular customers?"

"No," she says, relieved at his casual manner. "No, I just work the street and bars. Maybe one or two guys have picked me up twice by chance, but I never make appointments or arrangements." And for no reason she adds, "I used to have a pimp, a long time ago, back in LA."

Together they stroke the silence.

"Sera," he starts, "I hope that you understand how I feel about this. First of all, you're welcome to my money. We can buy a couple of cases of liquor and you can have the rest. But I don't think you're talking to me right now about money. I think you're talking about you. I'll tell you right now that I'm in love with you, but be that as it may, I'm not here to impose my twisted life on your soul. I'm not here to demand all your attentions, to the point where you're removed from your own life. We know I'm a drunk. That's part of what we have here, and you're all right with that. Likewise, we know you're a hooker, so if and when you decide to work, whatever your motivation, that's up to you. I don't think I'm inferring too much when I say that you've been doing this for long time, that you're comfortable with it. It's not as if you're a fifteen year old who's being victimized on the streets of Hollywood. I hope you understand that I'm a person who is totally at ease with this. You're not an oddity to me. In fact, I feel rather akin to you. Please don't think that my apparent indifference means that I don't care, I do. It simply means that I trust and accept your judgment, your inclinations. What I'm saying is: I hope that you understand that I understand."

His speech touches her, she likes it, and marvels at his ability to talk right to her, so eloquently, just minutes after being passed out drunk. "Thanks," she says. "I do understand. I was worried about how that would be, but now I'm not. And, you should know that included with the rent around here is a complimentary blowjob."

"Yes," he says thoughtfully, allowing her joke to tag a new

topic. "I suppose that sooner or later we ought to fuck."

"Whatever *that* means," she says. "Open your presents."

But he is not finished. Leaning back, he says, "Once I got beat up in a cathouse. Not that it has anything to do with what we were saying, but I'm reminded of it for some reason. I was in New York, about fifteen years old. My family was visiting relatives in Connecticut and I took the train into the city with my uncle. He went to work, and I got to spend the day roaming around New York City. All along I had it in the back of my head that I was going to find a hooker. I was still a virgin, but that's incidental; I would have had the same plan in any case. On Times Square I was given a handbill that described just what I was looking for, so I went to the address. Of course at that time I didn't know how things worked, and I happily laid down almost all my money— maybe twenty dollars—at the door, thinking that I was paying for everything. But once inside the room with the girl, after she explained to me how the tipping works, I realized that not only was I not gonna get laid, but I had also thrown away twenty dollars, a fair amount of money to me then. On my way out, less than five minutes since my arrival, I asked for my twenty back. Even the girl came out and tried to help me, but I could tell that she knew it was a lost cause. After all, these guys weren't running a non-profit organization. So they told me how it was and the guy gets up from behind the desk and grabs my collar—you know how bouncers push you by your neck—and shoves me to the door, which was at the top of a staircase. The place was just a little hole on a second story. At the door he said goodbye and let go of my collar. I was so outraged at my own ineptitude that I got crazy and tried to run back to the desk to take my money. It was stupid, but that's what I did. Needless to say, he had me again before I had taken a step. He just held me at arm's length with one hand and slapped me back and forth with the other. I woke up very sore at the bottom of the steps. I'm sure he carried me down, I can't imagine that he would have risked pushing me. Anyway, he knew what he was doing, because all I had was a bloody nose. The funny part is that I wanted terribly to go back up, not for my money, but to learn what these guys seemed to know. I wanted to be a sleazeball apprentice or something. I knew there was a world of experience in that dirty place that I could never share, and it pissed me off. I was consumed with envy.

"Now I'm softer. I know enough about all of it. Last spring I happened to walk past a house in LA that I had once patronized. There was a cool breeze off the ocean, and in the window I could see a woman's bare leg. She must have been relaxing, taking a break between customers. The moment set a mood for me and I paused on the sidewalk though I had to be somewhere else and was running late. I was reminded of myself as a very young boy being forced outside to play in the hot sun by my mother. Even though our house was cool, shady and comfortable, my mother felt it unhealthy for me to remain inside on a summer day. I'd stay inside as long as I could, keeping a low profile, until she would finally hear the other kids shouting and playing. That would be the last straw, and I found myself banished to the backyard, where I would look back in longing at the latched screen door. That was the exact feeling that I recaptured, looking at the hooker's leg in the window that day. The trees rustled in the breeze and I went up the walk. I felt very strongly, at that moment, that I belonged in that cathouse. I mention it as an epilogue to the other story. It was then that I had come full circle." A little embarrassed that he may be talking too much, he says, "I guess I better open my presents."

"Where is the house? The one in LA, I mean." He tells her and she knows it. One of Al's later girls had worked in that house; in fact, she claimed to have worked in a lot of houses, some very high pressure, some no longer around. Sera wonders if Ben ever clipped her. "Open this first," she says, handing him the larger of the two gifts.

Always uncomfortable when receiving presents, or, more accurately, uncomfortable when presented with hard evidence that anyone would want to give him something, Ben reluctantly takes the package and unwraps it.

"Very nice," he says, genuinely pleased as he holds the brightly colored shirt up to his chest. "This should work well with my suit." And indeed, it does seem to complement the black suit he is wearing. "You know, this suit is the only clothing that I brought over from the motel. The shirt is a nice start, but I thought we could do some shopping eventually. It might be fun."

"Of course," she says, thinking it through. "I didn't think about it before, but your suitcase must be full of liquor. You wouldn't leave that behind. But what about the clothes? Where are they?... You threw them out, right?"

"That's good," he says, amused at following her thought process. "When living with a drunk it's good to get in the habit of answering your own questions. I put them in the garbage behind the motel. But now that you mention it, I think that may have been a bit wasteful. I should have dropped them at some charity or left them on the street for the vagrants. In any case, they're gone. I thought it would be a sort of cleansing. Except for what I'm wearing and that suitcase itself, that was the last of my stuff from LA. I feel lighter. It's a good way for me to come to you, to your place."

"Nice talk," she says, and there is no sarcasm. "Keep drinking, Ben. It makes some interesting words fall from your mouth." Then, with a smile, "They must slip out between the one-hundred-and-one-proof breath and the occasional drool. Now try this one." She hands him the remaining gift and sits back to gauge his reaction.

"Well," he says simply, after opening the flask, "It looks like I'm with the right girl." Turning it in his hands, he pauses to assemble his words. "I must say I'm rather impressed that you would buy this for me. I know it wasn't done without some deliberation. Funny—how you did what I would have done." He tries the flask in his pocket and, satisfied with the fit, goes into the kitchen to fill it.

"Do you want to do some gambling tonight?" she calls after him. "We could go out and play for a few hours."

Returning to the room, he pulls his new flask out of his suit pocket and takes a drink, demonstrating its usefulness to her. He replaces it and smacks his lips, pats his chest with his open palm.

"I hadn't planned to do much gambling, but if you'll keep the bulk of my money here for me, I guess I can safely blow a couple of hundred bucks." He reaches for his folded stack of bills and peels off two hundreds, then a third. Returning the three bills to his pocket, he hands the balance to Sera. "Giving you money makes me want to come," he says.

Not sure how to take that, she takes it. "Then come. I'm going to change. Watch TV. I'll be ready in half an hour." She disappears into her bedroom.

He laughs to himself, thinking that she sounded ever-so-slightly offended by his stupid remark. Or perhaps the edge to her voice was an invitation to her bed, a frightening thought indeed, for in the back of his head is the nagging suspicion that his capacity for passionate lovemaking has been washed away in a tide of liquor and decline. Too much time spent looking in the mirror on the other side of the bar has revealed an image of a smelly, bloated, exhaustible, sick, self-indulgent man—not the sort of man who incites concupiscence in a woman, certainly not the sort of man who satisfies it. He listens to Sera's movements in the bedroom and thinks about his myriad deficiencies. They will become graffiti on her wall, ever larger and more intrusive as their lovemaking becomes habitual. The more he drinks, the worse it will get. He'll probably be dead long before she realizes that the evening's sex is over.

Ironically, though, he does want to come. His own quip has reminded him that it has been a while since he ejaculated; staying with Sera, he hasn't been jerking off lately. He had planned to do it when he was alone at the motel but ended up forgetting. Suddenly he is preoccupied with it; he wants to come right now. The sound of running water indicates that she is busy in the bathroom, so he takes out his handkerchief and undoes his pants. Slowly, silently, he masturbates in her living room. He fantasizes about picking up a hooker tomorrow night when she is out working and, on that thought, comes painfully into his own hand.

"I'm ready," she says, emerging from the bedroom fifteen minutes later. She wears a pale green summer dress: tasteful. Her hair falls freely, frames two mismatched earrings that nonetheless complement each other.

"I like your earrings," he says. He has had time to put on his new shirt, which he wears under his suit. Were he harsher in the face he might look like a retired drug dealer, if there is such a thing. As it is, he looks good but slightly off balance. In fact he is off balance, having polished off the initial filling of his flask in order to embark on the evening's activities armed with a fully loaded vessel. "I like women who wear mismatched earrings."

"Well then, let's hope that we don't run into any tonight. I do expect some sort of loyalty here. Just because I fuck for money doesn't give you cause to start picking up women and leaving me looking silly." She holds her eyes firmly, and they seem to veto the smile that sits beneath them. A technical jest that is an actual law, this is true communication, a woman at her finest.

"I only have eyes for you,... and we both know that you would never become romantically involved with a trick," he says as he stands up.

She follows him into the kitchen, where he refills his flask and she phones for a cab. Turning out the light, they go out to the street and wait for the cab, which only takes a minute to arrive and collect them.

They are whisked to the Strip and in no time find themselves walking through the crowd and clamor of a hotel casino. Smoke fills the room and diminishes Ben's depth perception so that he sees compressed montages of green felt littered with mottled chips, of ice filled glasses on glass filled trays, of ass-filled panties and tit-filled bras, and more cleavage than would seem probable in a species at this advanced stage of its evolution. Cocktail waitresses and keno girls wear costumes that flirt at inadequacy and lick his eyes with the promise of a stray pubic hair or a poorly concealed nipple. Country boys on vacation wear athletic tee shirts and fine gold chains around their necks. Trying to look intimidating despite their intimidation, they glare from behind their moustaches and hope that their bright-eyed, busty girl-friends don't wonder too much what it would be like to bear a bit of unfamiliar semen back home, packed up somewhere between those milky midwestern thighs. The floormen wear suits and expressions of feigned usefulness. The place pops with quick detonations of elation and anguish, money won and lost. The ceiling spits light and pretends not to know about the cameras that it not-so-secretly dangles. Security men crawl like cock-roaches on catwalks hidden behind one-way mirrors. Chrome hemispheres eye the room tirelessly, showing it back to itself again, ever-so-briefly after it first happens: a light jump away. The outcome of each bet is decided before the evidence reaches anybody's eyes, a quantum of radiant energy.

Ben absorbs what he can from the abundance of energy that surrounds him and uses it like a stimulant, now as a body charge and later, hopefully, to cheat himself into more liquor. Pushing Sera roughly against a slot machine, he kisses her deeply. Her first instinct is to resist, then to succumb as a means of self-preservation, and finally, after he eases up in reaction to the sound of change knocked over by her hip, she remembers that she has nothing to fear from this man, and succumbs as a natural segment of passion. He licks her cheek and pulls away. With the occasional, surprising dexterity of the always drunk, he stoops and collects the spilled quarters in one motion, stands and returns them to the entertained slot-machine player, who then goes back to his previous diversion. Ben grabs Sera's arm and, with a healthy trot, leads her towards the bar. She keeps pace, happy in her heart with this quick upswing, admitting to herself the theatrical appeal of this alcoholic. Her life has had so little entertainment, and she digs the drama as well as the drunk. Anyway, he needs her, and for that, she loves him.

♣　♣　♣

The sonic boom of an Air Force jet passing in the desert serves as the reference point at which Ben's memory resumes its record. From his vantage point on Sera's living room floor he can see, through the top of the window, that it is still dark outside but won't be for long. Since he feels all right physically he knows that he has only been down for a few hours. Nonetheless, his first move is to a vodka bottle which he senses on the kitchen table. Starting on all fours and gradually rising to a slouch, he makes his way to the kitchen, where he pours eight ounces of vodka and two ounces of orange soda into a dirty tumbler. He downs the warm mixture in less than a minute and waits over the sink, ready should his stomach reject the elixir. Satisfied that he'll be able to hold it down, and instantly feeling on his way up, he steps quietly into Sera's bedroom and eases next to her, on top of the sheet that covers her.

She turns her head, opens her eyes, and looks at him. "How are you doing?" she asks.

"Very well…. Umm, I never expected anyone to have to do this for me again, but could you tell me how our evening went? I blacked out about the time we got to the casino. I can't remember any of it." Despite the severe independence that he has gained by planning his own demise, he can't help but feel the same old guilt that he used to know when he would pose similar requests to his wife. Back then he was truly interested in her answer, but he has long since become bored with these recaps. Now, it's not so much that he cares about what he did last night, but more that he needs to find out how Sera feels about what he did, how Sera feels about him.

"It wasn't so bad. I guess I would have been prepared for worse. We were sitting at the bar talking about blackjack. You seemed just fine—a little drunker than usual, but nothing really strange. Then I noticed your head start to droop, so I put my hand on your shoulder. Wham! You swung your arm at me and jumped back, falling off the barstool and crashing into a cocktail waitress. Her tray was full when you hit her, so there was a terrible mess. You were yelling *Fuck!* over and over again, very loudly. I tried to shut you up and help you to your feet, but you kept swinging at me—not so much like you wanted to hit me, but more just waving me away. Security was there by then and you stopped yelling when you saw them. They weren't sure what to do. They said they were going to carry you out and dump you on the street, but they didn't move. It's probably a standard bluff. Things started to settle down, and I talked them into letting me walk you out."

"What did you tell them?"

She looks at him flatly. "That you were an alcoholic and I would take you home. I also promised that you would never walk in there again."

He nods and smiles for lack of a better reaction. "What happened next?" he asks.

"You were acting okay, so we walked for about a block. Then you said that you wanted to go home and fuck, but I think that even you knew that that wasn't going to happen. We got a cab for home. You made us stop at a liquor store, though I tried to tell you that there was still plenty here. Oh yeah! I almost forgot. At the liquor store you got two bottles of vodka. It came to just over twenty bucks, and you gave the kid a hundred and told him to keep the change. I asked you if you knew it was a hundred dollar bill. You said you did, so I let you do it. Anyway, we got home, you made us some drinks, and ten minutes later you were asleep on the floor. I covered you up and came to bed."

"I warned you. I'm sorry," he says sincerely.

"Here's my speech. I know that this shouldn't be acceptable to me, but it is. Don't ask me to explain. Maybe I'm not doing what I should be, but I think I'm doing what you need me to do. I sense that your trouble is very big, and I'm scared for you. But falling down in a casino is little stuff. It doesn't bother me. It has nothing to do with us."

"That's amazing," he says, truly impressed. "What are you, some sort of angel visiting me from one of my drunk fantasies? How can you be so old?"

She turns away on the pillow and says to the wall, "I don't

know what you're saying. I'm just using you. I need you. Can we not talk about it anymore. Please, not another word, okay?"

He strokes her back absently, reviewing this, lost in his own thoughts and feeling the gathering calm as the alcohol enters his blood in force. "Why don't you go back to sleep. I'll go out and buy you some breakfast."

"Be careful," she says.

"Don't worry." Standing, he walks to the door.

She calls after him, "Ben, I'm working tonight."

"I know," he says, and goes to the kitchen, where he splashes water on his face and drinks another tumbler of vodka.

The first stop on the way to the grocery store, which is nearby but not yet open, is a small casino-restaurant-bar, which is not so nearby but always open. He pays the cab and enters the building, passing through a glass door and a tattered red velvet curtain which lies behind it. The bar, dirty, dark, and instantly familiar, is just what he had in mind; this place has outlived more than a few of its regulars. A man sleeps at one end, his face in a puddle of spilled beer. A middle-aged woman in hot pants dances alone at the jukebox. Ben takes his place on a chrome-legged stool with a black vinyl top. Behind him eight slot machines wait to be handled; two blackjack tables wait to be uncovered; the morning cook waits for any orders that may be forthcoming. The bartender bids Ben good morning and slaps a cocktail napkin down in front of him. He asks for a beer and a double kamikaze; the bartender nods. Sitting at a table in the back of the room, a biker couple argues with slurred words and non sequiturs. *Get Up, Las Vegas!* is airing live on a silent television which hangs over the liquor bottles.

His plan, his reason for being here, is to make Sera feel a little bit better about him. He'll first drink himself sober at the bar, starting with kamikazes and moving into bloody marys. Next, he'll try to eat some saltine crackers, and if that goes well, he can try to get down an egg and some toast as a way to prepare his stomach for the impending unpleasantness. Then he'll go home with a sack of groceries and make them both breakfast. A perfect balance gets more difficult to strike with each new day, but if he handles all these preliminaries properly, he should be able to eat an actual breakfast, his second, in front of her. This is a trick that she hasn't yet seen, in fact, she hasn't seen him eat a single meal since they've been together, and it should allay some of her fears about his condition.

Still wearing his suit and the shirt that she bought him, he is fifteen minutes into his kamikazes when the better half of the motorcycle couple comes and presses up to him.

"Why are you all dressed up, honey? Don't you look fine," she says, with her cheek on his arm. She looks up to him and outlines her mouth with her tongue. "I am very bored with my date. Would you like to buy me a drink?"

Trapped, he looks over to her friend, across the room. The man is big, drunk, and probably witless. Against his better judgment, but seeing no other way, he says loudly, "Do you mind if I buy her a drink?"

"Fuck her. I don't care what the fuck you do with her," he replies, glaring.

"Maybe I could buy you both a drink?" tries Ben.

"Fuck you. Don't fuck with me, motherfucker. Fuck off. Leave me alone. Go to it, she's waitin' for her drink." He stands, walks over to a slot machine, and drops in a quarter, never taking his eyes off of Ben and the girl.

"See what an asshole he is," says the girl. "I'll have a rum and coke." And she smiles her best smile.

He orders the drink as the girl moves closer and puts her hand on his crotch.

"Can I come stay with you for a while?" she asks.

"You mean move in with me? Isn't this rather sudden?" he says, going along.

But she thinks she is serious, at least she is for the moment. "Oh, I don't have a lot of stuff."

"I don't think my wife would dig it too much," he says, instantly pleased with the facile lie. He looks over to her friend, who is still watching them, and feels himself standing on the edge of a chasm.

"Well," she says, nuzzling up to his ear and sucking on the lobe, "maybe we could just go find a room and fuck all day. You wouldn't have to tell your wife about that, now would you?"

Ben looks down at her fuck-me eyes and evaluates her. Clearly, she is doing this for the benefit of her companion, still lurking behind them. But it doesn't end there; he can see that this is the sort of thing she enjoys, that if he were to walk out with her she would be very happy to follow through with her part, perhaps looking forward to the beating that she would ultimately face when, later that night, she caught up with her friend.

He thinks about Sera and how good she has been to him. He simply cannot imagine a woman that he would rather be with.

Suddenly, the biker throws down his beer can and comes marching across the room. "Now listen, motherfucker," he says loudly, grabbing Ben's shoulder and turning him around on his stool. "I'm not gonna sit here and watch her suck on your ear. Now, I know that she came over to you—she does that a lot—so I'm gonna pretend that you're innocent and give you one chance to walk out of this place. Right Now!" He looks at Ben, close and hard, with eyes full of alcohol, fury, and pain.

Behind his own eyes, Ben must admit that he is impressed by the man's attitude. He would not have guessed the man capable of this sort of rational self-control, such as it is.

He shakes his arm free of the man's grip and says, "I'm sorry, but she and I have decided to spend a few hours together."

Not being a fighter, Ben is amazed, not at the fact, but at the swiftness of the first punch, which, delivered to his jaw, sends him and his stool crashing to the dirty floor. No sooner does his head crack against the tile than he is lifted again and feels a fist skim across his face, crunching his nose and spraying blood into his eyes. He falls again to the floor, where he tries to hang on to consciousness, and listens to their footsteps as they vanish out the door.

Then the bartender is over him with a wet towel. He has seen this sort of thing many times before, so he is not without experience. "You're quite a fighter," he says, his voice laced with friendly sarcasm. He helps Ben back up and wipes his face, goes behind the bar, wets another towel, and makes another kamikaze. "Here's a drink on me, but then I'm going to have to ask you to leave. It may sound silly in your case, but that's what we do when there's a fight here. Men's room is in the back." And he goes back to washing glasses.

After drinking and cleaning up, Ben takes a cab to the grocery store, and arrives home carrying a sack, still determined to eat what he can in front of Sera. He finds her reading on the couch.

"I'm back." Putting the bag in the kitchen, he goes to kiss her.

"Oh no!" she says, seeing his face and dropping her book. "Oh fuck, Ben, look at your face. You got in a fight, I thought you didn't fight. Goddammit. How do you feel?" Not waiting for his response, she disappears into the bathroom, returning with towels, tissues, and medicinal looking bottles. A little calmer, and reacting to his smile, she says, "What happened? Muggees normally don't walk around so happy. Of course I knew that you would stop at a bar. Did you say something stupid to someone stupid?" She shifts into nurse mode and goes to work on his face.

"Absolutely not," he says. "I was defending the honor of some poor wayward maiden."

She stops to read this, and swallows it without comment. Stinging an open cut with a dab of Mercurochrome, she says, "Why don't you go finish this up in the bathroom. Shower and put on your other shirt. I'll make breakfast, and then we'll go out and buy you some clothes. I think that suit is unlucky." She playfully tosses a wet rag at him and, with a critical look, kisses his forehead. He watches as she walks away, shaking her head.

In the bathroom, standing in front of the mirror, he looks at his now slightly-crooked nose, his bruised, swollen, and cut cheek, his puffy eye. His fingers find the rising bump on the back of his head, causing him to wince as they inspect it. He smiles widely, spins on his heel, and, laughing to himself, takes the first sip of a freshly made drink, and starts the shower.

The day ticks on; Ben strikes and savors a high point. Without thinking too much about why, he knows that he's pretty damn happy and will stay that way for at least the next few hours. So, counting on a fuckupless afternoon, he endeavors to brighten and entertain Sera with gifts and more-carefully-timed drinks during their little shopping trip. Initially, he is resolved to acquiesce to whatever fashion choices she cares to make for him, but in the stores he feels a little more conservative, and finally decides on a pair of black jeans and two white dress shirts. As a compromise, the socks are chosen for their improbable colors and patterns.

"Very creative," she says. "Now we'll get you a black bow tie, and you can look just like one of the casino dealers."

"No," he says. "The dealers wear this stuff because they're told to; I wear it because I want to. That makes me look different."

They are sitting in one of the less objectionable restaurants of the shopping mall, reviewing the day's purchases. It has indeed been a fun afternoon for Sera, and though she finds the marks on Ben's face deeply disturbing, almost an evil portent that she can't quite dismiss, she is willing to pretend that her anxiety is due mostly to her own recent beating, still very clear in her mind. She marvels at his feigned normalcy. He can be so high and happy, so able to ignore the cloud that seems to loom just above his head. He drinks amazing quantities with apparent impunity, then disregards the obvious punition. Tossing down her tequila, she embraces, as he makes it so easy for her to do, the wellness of prosaic laughter, and reaches across the table to accept the small box that he is holding out to her.

"There was no time for me to have it wrapped," he says, "with you breathing down my neck all day. So you'll have to wing it, baby." An attempt to chuckle brings on, instead, a fit of coughing followed by a rush of nausea, which he suppresses, though not without some difficulty. Downing the balance of his drink, he calls for another and immediately tries to move things along as if nothing has happened. "I think you'll find it rather easy to open."

She follows his prompt and snaps open the box, revealing a pair of black onyx earrings set in white gold.

"Your color," she says, though she is obviously pleased.

"I think you should wear one at a time—one of those, and some other earring on the other ear. In fact I would have bought just one, but I didn't think it would fly... as a gift, I mean." His new drink arrives and he takes a deep swallow, then another.

"I'll wear them tonight. I'll wear one of them tonight," she says. At first she thinks that she may have made a tactless slip, as she is planning to work tonight. But then she relaxes, recalling that this issue, when last discussed, was left on a comfortable note.

But Ben has one of those moments that are the liability of any drunk, when the meaning that he is attempting to convey is mismatched with unfortunate words, and by the time the whole thing leaves his mouth even he is unsure of what he feels.

"Yes," he says, looking into his again empty glass, "you'll be able to feel it sharp and hot under your ear as one of the brothers is driving your head, face down, into a penthouse pillow." He tries to look grim, but he is shocked at his own remark. Realizing that she does not deserve this, yet nonetheless disturbed by the image, he stands and walks quickly from the table, unable to bear her gaze.

"Ben, wait!" she calls after him. She fumbles with her purse, trying to leave money for the check. "Please, wait for me."

When Ben reaches the door, a large Black man steps into his path and places his hands on Ben's shoulders. "Maybe you should wait for her," says the man.

"Why," says Ben, trying unsuccessfully to shake himself loose from the grip.

The man pauses, as if searching for words that Ben will understand. "Because," he says, "you can hear in her voice that she really wants you to."

As Sera catches up to them, the man lets go of Ben and steps aside. Ben takes up the packages from her, and they step out to the mall.

"What was that? I don't understand any of that," she says.

"Can we forget it?" he says, imploring. "Can we just ignore it?"

The mall's public address is yakking inanely above them. Ben looks back at the interloper in the restaurant, and sees him walking into the men's room.

"Yes," says Sera, "I'll give you that." And she does.

That night, as Ben drinks bourbon in the silent kitchen, waiting for his use, in turn, of the apartment's single bathroom and shower, Sera delivers herself to the temporary solitude of her bedroom and prepares to repair to the streets, bars, and hotel rooms of Las Vegas. In her room, at her mirror, she finds that each familiar action has changed slightly, has slipped sideways into a new light, a new meaning. This will be the first time that she goes to work and leaves a man waiting for her at home—a man whom she wants to come home to—and though she finds herself very attached to him, she is looking forward to this time alone with her regular life, this somewhat defiant break. It's getting hard to watch him, and she could stand a dose of pain on her own terms— the addict's thrill of the self-administered injection, sometimes performed just for the sensory sting, long after the heroin has run out. Her face, oddly, has never shown the miles; at least she doesn't look as hard as most girls. There is only the scar from Al's ring, now trying out its final form on her cheek and behind her eyes. A heavy lick of really red lipstick, a double slash of black mascara, everything is a bit overdone this time. Clear cut boundaries overcome the thin lines. A long time actress, now she's playing for an audience that will never see the show, but this she does not realize. Here, as she flips off the bedroom light out of habit, then back on, remembering that he will be using the room to change for his own treacherous evening, she stops, and, in the flash, catches a real glimpse in the mirror of a hooker and a girl. She doesn't dare think of what it would be like to not have to work.

"I'll be home around two or three. If you're back by then we can watch TV or something," she says, bending to kiss him. "I guess I'm saying that I hope you'll be home when I get home, but in any case, whatever you end up doing," this with a raised eyebrow, "please be careful."

"Don't worry about me, Sera. God watches over the likes of me. You know that." He laughs under his breath, having never been able to decide if the old saying is ridiculous or obvious. "Seriously, ninety-nine percent of my feeling about this is concern for your well-being. The rest is... I guess it's plain old separation anxiety. I'm going to miss you."

Wrapping up her goodbye kiss, she says, "See you later," and opens the door.

"Maybe I should follow you and ask one of your tricks what it's like to sleep with you," he says in good humor.

"They wouldn't know. Maybe you should just ask me sometime. I'd be happy to show you." She shoots him a lusty little glance, and, in a sequin's flash, is gone.

"Fuck!" he says aloud to himself, "there sure is a lot of biology in that girl." He finds this line so amusing that he laughs aloud, alone in the kitchen, until a fit of coughing takes over, and he vomits in the sink.

But later, after he has cleaned up, dressed, and drunk to replace the liquor that he lost to the plumbing, he starts laughing again. He continues to laugh, under the dark sky, as he staggers down the street, falls, gets up and staggers on.

♣  ♣  ♣

At this late date The Grand Canyon really doesn't hold their interest, barely even qualifies as a part of the scenery, has even less relevance than an antique, having not been wrought by intelligent hands. Lake Mead, however, sloshing around in the bottom of that big hole, is a human doodle in the dust, a by-product of boredom and dissatisfaction. Ben and Sera run, splashing into the water, and though the bottom—once desert and still refusing to accept its new role—is rocky, the cool water is as right as anything could be, righter than water should be: this is where you live, because this is what you built.

Ninety meters behind them, the red rental car bakes in the sun. Thirty miles beyond that lies Las Vegas, where fourteen hours ago, Sera wrapped up the last trick of her first night's work since Ben moved in. She had come home tired, but both she and Ben were in good spirits, as if a slight readjustment had finally been made to a machine that everyone thought was running just fine, causing in it a pleasant but unexpected improvement. A chunk of ground was regained, a die was cast; nothing almost didn't happen, and then didn't happen anyway. Sera had a good night on her own terms and felt like blowing some money. Ben readily agreed.

"Let's go out of town," he said. "We'll rent a car and drive to the dam, or wherever. Not far. Be back before you know it. A cheap tourist motel with a pool. One night out of town. What do you say?" Inexplicably overly enthused, he beamed at her nod and bounced to the kitchen for a beer.

Now he swims up to her, secretly out of breath, in search of a more accommodating depth, and says, "So we'll stay in Boulder City tonight?"

"There's no gambling there, no casinos," she says. "I don't think that they stay awake all night and drink there."

"I know. We could go to a movie, then go to a bar, one that actually closes, and not listen to slot machines."

"This doesn't sound like you," she says, laughing. "Okay, let's go. I want to get there and get a room before it's too late to swim. I feel like swimming in a real pool."

"This is a real pool," he says, splashing her.

In Boulder City they find a nice little motel and pool. Mostly occupied by the not-quite-so-transient, the place offers kitchen-ettes and weekly rates, neither of which are elected by Sera and Ben. They end up in a converted storeroom behind the office, choosing it not so much for the reduced rate as for the unique layout of the floor and walls. It is the sort of space that can be found in oddly designed buildings, a little leftover part of the world that ends up enclosed between the more intentional de-signs that are built around it. Sera quickly puts on her bathing suit and runs out to the pool to catch the late afternoon sun. Ben, still wearing the new drugstore shorts that he wore in Lake Mead, unpacks the liquor that was purchased at the same store. Care-fully he sets up his bar on the nightstand: two fifths of bourbon, one each vodka and tequila. He fills the ice bucket: *For Our Guests*, pours a Lake Mead souvenir glass full of tequila and orange juice for Sera, and, carrying a bottle of Wild Turkey for himself, goes out to join her.

"I've missed the best sun," she says, pouting. "Why did you have to pawn your watch?"

"Because I didn't know that I would be taking you swimming in Boulder City, of course. Sera, you must be joking. You're telling me that you need a watch to tell you the position of the sun? We've been driving in the desert all day. You only had to look up to see how much sun was left." He hands her the drink and drops into a basket chair next to her, all more quickly than he had planned, having, at the last moment, lost his balance.

"That doesn't do me any good. I need to know what time it is so I can tell when the best sun is out."

"No, actually, you need to know where the sun is in order to know what time it is."

She frowns at the cement, then, seeing what he is getting at, laughs and says, "Wake up, drunk man! If the sun burned out tomorrow, and we could somehow stay warm, the clocks wouldn't stop. Check-out time would still be 11:00 a.m.."

"Don't fuck with me," he says, and pours some bourbon into his mouth. He enjoys this familiar banter that they have been slipping into lately, enjoys topics that exist outside of themselves.

"Let me taste that," she says, indicating with her outstretched arm the bottle of Wild Turkey.

He hands it to her and watches in admiration as she easily swallows a mouthful. She returns the bottle to him and walks to the weather-beaten diving board. Unaccustomed to being mounted by a full grown woman, the board creaks and pops in protest as she bounces to the end and feels for the reluctant spring. She is determined to follow through with or without the springboard's help, and snapping her hiked up suit out from between her legs, as women will, she plunges into the water with the unstudied grace of the natural athlete she is. When she emerges, Ben toasts her by holding high, then drinking deeply from the bourbon bottle. She walks back to him and, dripping cold water on his chest, bends to kiss him.

On her breath he can taste the bourbon that she drank. It tastes different, yet complements well the swallow that he, himself, has just taken. Planning to demonstrate his own diving skills, he stands, and immediately slips on the wet cement. Without the capacity for quick recovery, he has pretty much doomed any slip that he might experience to becoming a fall, and so it is with this one. It is a magnificent fall, partially into the chair, which, none-to-steady to begin with, crumbles irreparably under him, and partially onto a small table containing Sera's glass. The glass as well as the bottle he was holding shatter dramatically, sending little bourbon and tequila-dipped missiles in all directions, mostly into the pool. Blood, thinned by the water already on the cement, is spreading in all directions from under him. Seeing this, Sera gasps, grabs her towel, and kneels to him. He sits up, pieces of glass sticking to his chest and arm, and smiles doubtfully at her.

"I guess I better go in and nap," he says. But, really, he is thinking about the replacement bottle of bourbon that sits next to the ice bucket on the nightstand.

"You're cut," she says, by now having learned to bypass worry and go directly to cleanup.

"I'll take care of it. Perhaps you could deal with this," he says, indicating the mess. He walks steadily to the room, proud of his growing collection of cuts, bruises, and scars.

Carrying a broom and dustpan, the desk clerk approaches Sera. "Everybody okay?" he asks cheerfully.

"Yes, fine," she says. "Don't worry, we'll pay for the chair, and I'll clean all this up, the pool too." She can't help but notice his happy demeanor and the matter-of-fact way that, ignoring her offer, he bends to the work. "You seem prepared for accidents."

He looks up at her, still smiling. "Yeah, we get a lot of fuck-ups around here. Now, you two keep your liquor and your loud talk in your room, and after you check out tomorrow morning I don't ever want to see you here again. Let's just leave it at that. I don't need you paying for the chair, or cutting your pretty hands on this glass. See ya' in the morning." Nodding firmly, he returns to the mess, indicating that the conversation is over.

"They're not real happy with us," Sera says, entering the room. "We're banished to our room." She pours herself a drink and sits next to him on the bed. "Are you okay? Any major cuts?"

He swallows from a plastic cup. There are a dozen or so tiny pieces of tissue stuck to his chest with clotting blood. "I must be indestructible. I'm surprised this stuff still clots after all the thinning. Anyway, I'm not taking any chances with my last bottle. I'm keeping it at least ten feet away from me and drinking out of these." He holds up the plastic cup. "We'll have to stop for more Turkey when we go out. I want to save the vodka for breakfast." After taking another sip, he relaxes back on the pillow and looks her over.

She is still in her bathing suit, and he is struck with how very desirable she is, how comely her body is. He's been telling himself over and over that they will make love soon; certainly she's been hinting at it, and he need only make an advance. But he knows better. He knows that he can barely muster the energy to roll over in bed anymore. His mastery of motor functions has all but disappeared. These days, it takes a minimum of one fifth of vodka just to brace his nerves for the trauma of standing upright out of bed, and half the time, when he's finally had enough to stand comfortably, he can no longer stand at all. He admires the resolution that she must have made to herself, how she fails to fuck with him about not fucking, indeed, how she fails to fuck with him about anything. Even as the test gets harder, and as she must be going places that she never thought she'd go, she still remains true. The implied terms have not escaped her, he thinks, the golden rule that even he no longer has the power to veto: there is nothing that will stop me from drinking.

But this insinuation of timidity cheapens her, cheapens the sublime act of selfish selflessness that she is prolonging; the basic loneliness of her humanity, and the knowing and accepting the conditions of that which has been shown to assuage it. Sera's not living up to any agreement, she is simply living. Ben gave this back to her, and therein lies the agreement.

She is glad to see that he has fallen asleep, for she felt herself on the verge of asking after his health, and it is a topic about which she would rather not be too well informed; as it is she can see far too much. When he awakens they will have a fun night together. He is consistent in his ability to deliver that much. She refills her cup and turns on the television. Lying next to him, she feels herself grow slightly intoxicated, and giggles quietly at a therefore entertaining sitcom.

♣  ♣  ♣

A slight vibration in the earth, real or imagined, pulls the thread of Ben's dream to Los Angeles, causing him to awaken with a start from his first long nap since they returned from Boulder City two days earlier. The nap, though, has been too long, and as he sits up in the bed, he realizes that he must act quickly if he is to prevent the imminent withdrawals from seizing control of his body. Already his hand shakes violently as he staggers to the kitchen for some vodka. Sera is standing over the stove.

"Hi," she says, and kisses his sweaty cheek. Sensing his condition, she turns back to her cooking. This is a performance that she finds too disquieting to watch. "You probably don't want to hear about it right now, but I bought some plain rice. I thought it might be something that you could eat. So if you get hungry later just let me know and I'll whip some up." She turns smiling, hand on her hip, in mock parody of her housewife role.

"Okay," he mutters. "I'm gonna get in the shower." And he staggers back out of the room, a fifth of vodka in each hand.

It is a rare, cloudy afternoon in Las Vegas, and the diffused sunlight is muddied even further by the translucence of the tiny bathroom window. The heavy sweat on his palms makes it difficult for him to keep a firm grip on the neck of the vodka bottle, but with two hands he is able to drink, then set it down without incident. Hunched over the sink with his hands now grasping the cold porcelain, he immediately vomits, as he knew he would, and tries again. Not until he opens the second bottle is he able to keep any of it in his stomach. Five minutes later, standing upright a little more firmly, he manages a quick shower, punctuated by carefully timed drinks. Thirty minutes after entering the bathroom, he emerges, carrying the two empties, feeling well enough to grin, and as ready as he can be for his first drink of the day.

"I think I'm ready for rice," he says, finding her still in the kitchen.

When he is dressed, sitting at her kitchen table, sipping alternately from a beer can and a glass of bourbon, she places a bowl of rice before him, and he obediently eats from it. Her own bowl, a rather more elaborate affair including vegetables and soy sauce, remains untouched. There is no conversation, and only an occasional passing car can be heard above the silence.

"You're pretty sick," she blurts out. "What are you gonna do?" She waits for a response, but gets only a stare. "I want you to go see a doctor." With this she folds her arms and continues to meet his eyes.

"Sera," he starts thoughtfully, "look, we've never really talked this over... well, I mean...." He stammers, searching for an explanation that sounds even remotely acceptable. "Sera, I'm not going to a doctor." And then, prepared, as he has been from the start, to burn this final bridge, he says, "Maybe it's time I moved to a hotel."

"And do what, rot away in a room? We're not going to talk about that! I will not talk about that! Fuck you! You're staying here. You are not moving to a hotel. One thing! This is one thing you can do for me. I've given you gallons of free will here, you can do this for me." She is outraged. Leaning forward, as if it constitutes her final argument, she says, "Let's face it. As sick as you are, I'm probably the only thing that's keeping you alive."

And Ben, though he offers no response, has to agree that this is true.

♣  ♣  ♣

Wandering the Strip that night, exceptionally far from the good judgment that he may have once been capable of, he makes a two hundred dollar bet at a craps table and wins. As he collects his chips he is simultaneously confronted with a glimpse of a leggy show girl, the sudden smack of a recently consumed double shot of bourbon, and an erection. In no time at all he is seated in the back of a cab bound for the apartment, an irresistible idea in his head and a pornographic circular in his lap.

He refuses to think about anything—blind but for the well placed, useful smells and sensations of liquor and pussy—as the cab, the universe, sweeps him down the short stretch of semi-highway that leads to his—her—bed. Sera is out working, will be for another hour or so. Might get interesting, he thinks, excess bourbon from a misjudged swill streaming down his chin. The cab arrives, and Ben returns the flask to his pocket, pays the fare and stumbles to the apartment.

Thumbing through the paper, he selects a quarter-page adver-tisement from the rear: A hand drawn girl on all fours advises, *Don't be alone in Las Vegas*. He makes the call, giving the address of the apartment, a vague request for expeditiousness, and a definite request for a girl that has had "a lot of use." After hanging up, he regrets this latter unfortunate phrase for its tactlessness, and hopes that it doesn't find its way to the subject's ears.

The girl, as it turns out when she knocks on the door, doesn't seem to be the sort that would care one way or another what Ben has to say about her. Big and busty, a would-be blond with an attitude that is pure, cold business, she pushes her way past Ben and looks curiously around the room.

"I need to call in and let them know that I got here, then we can talk. I also need a hundred dollars up front. That's the service's fee—I don't see any of that—and I need to tell them that you've paid it, or they'll tell me to leave," she says.

He dutifully peels off a hundred, hands it to her, and shows her the phone. While she is calling, he pours himself a glass of bourbon, and takes it, with the bottle, to the bedroom. When he returns she is done with her call.

"I need," he starts, mocking her, his voice thick with liquor, "to fuck you for an hour." Satisfied, in his alcoholic haze, that he has just made an attractive offer, he drops into a chair, grins and folds his arms.

"Straight fuck is two hundred, but I doubt that you'll be awake for an hour."

"How mush to lick your pussy," he slurs.

"Sorry," she says, pleased at this opportunity to refuse him something, "only my boyfriend can do that."

Not having the energy for even the smallest debate, he swallows this, though he is disappointed, and gives her three more hundreds, saying, "Your tip in advance. Bed's in here."

The hooker is on top, suspecting, by his diminishing penis inside of her, that he has fallen asleep, which he very nearly has, when Sera, turning on the light, enters her bedroom. Sera winces at the picture, then immediately seizes her composure. She looks expectantly at the hooker, who, in one continuous motion, gets off of Ben, pulls on her dress, and silently walks past her and out the front door. Sera looks at Ben, and a tear grows in her eye.

"There are limits," she says.

"Yes," he says, sobering slightly, "I guess I knew that."

She drops her purse and collapses against the wall, coming to rest seated on the floor, weeping quietly.

Then, claiming his prize, he says, "Perhaps I could crash on the couch for a few hours before looking for a room." He picks up his bottle and walks out to the couch, where he hears no argument, only the sound of her bedroom door closing.

♣　♣　♣

The room, dark though it is midday, is thick with the smell of liquor and the taste of atrophy. She presses inward, behind his naked body as it retreats to the bed after answering her knock. It has been twelve days since they have seen each other, twelve days between the morning that he left her apartment and his phone call an hour ago.

"Ben," she says, sitting on the bed. But the scene is too far removed from her experience, too low, and she is at a loss for words. She strokes his sweaty forehead. "Have you been in here since you left? It smells awful. It's so dark." Leaning forward, she turns on the nightstand lamp, and is stunned by his appearance. "Oh, Ben, you look so very sick. You're so pale. Wait here." Rising, she goes to the bathroom and wets a washcloth to wipe his face.

"I wanted to see you," he says. He is very drunk; he is, in fact, very much beyond drunk. Punctuated by frequent coughs and gasps, occasionally blocked by mucous, his broken speech is difficult to understand, difficult, even, to listen to. "...called you to see you." After several unsuccessful attempts, he manages to sit up in the bed and, producing a bottle from under the sheet, drinks instinctively.

Sera, stepping out of the bathroom, stops and watches, impressed at the fluid skill of this one action, the strange precision that seems to guide his hand for this single task, when everything else about him, even his breathing, is inept. Sitting again on the bed, she wipes the sweat and dirt from his face, which vaguely smiles in acknowledgement, and stares across the room at the drawn drape.

"I'm sorry I put us asunder," he says, tears welling up in his eyes, and drinks again from the bottle.

Too close to the source of her pain, she repairs to the window, where she draws the floral drapery. There is a balcony, so she opens the glass door and sits—half inside, half outside—and looks out onto the Strip, the desert. But after a few moments, the distant sounds of traffic and wind are augmented by a rhythmic creaking from the bed, and turning, she sees that he has thrown the sheet off of himself and is masturbating furiously. She returns to the bed, but he doesn't seem to know that she is there. The tears are now streaming down either side of his face.

"Why don't you let me do that," she says, covering his hand with hers.

Silently withdrawing his hands, he clutches her thigh, and she takes up gently, expertly the motion. Eventually—she has no idea how much later, for her hand is tireless and her emotions over-flowing—he ejaculates, and she falls prone at his side, on the bed, where they both escape to separate dreams.

She awakens to the sound of a gasp. One of his frequent muscle spasms jolts the bed, and she finds him staring out the now dark window, blinking his eyes.

"Ben," she says, "do you want me to help you?"

He mutters what sounds like *no* and begins searching the bed for his bottle. Unable to watch him drink another swallow, she stands and walks to the open window.

(She caught a glimpse of him in the kitchen on their second night together. She couldn't believe his posture, the intensity with which he winced as he drained the bottle.

He trembled with pain, eyes squeezed tightly closed; then they opened and saw her. "Oh," he said. "I'm sorry." He smiled awkwardly, reddened and turned away so that she might vanish and never mention it.

She never did.)

A siren is screaming down the Strip. Red lights flashing, it is a surprisingly rare sight for such an alive and therefore precarious place. When the sound fades it is replaced by nothing, nothing.

("That's amazing," he said, truly impressed. "What are you, some sort of angel visiting me from one of my drunk fantasies? How can you be so old?"

She turned away on the pillow and said to the wall, "I don't know what you're saying. I'm just using you. I need you. Can we not talk about it anymore. Please, not another word, okay?")

Suddenly feeling the vacuum in the room, petrified by relief and sorrow, exhausted by reality, she knows, even before she turns and sees his still body, that he is gone.

("Quiet," he said, resting his hand over her mouth. "Try not to be so consumed with the future."

But Sera hadn't felt the future at all, for it wasn't until that moment, laden with his words and redolent with his prescience, that she too knew what would come to pass. It all became clear, how much more deliberate his life was than hers, how he knew the one great trick that she couldn't do, and how she would fall in love with him every minute, every second, over and over again, for the rest of her life.)

And his lifeless body grows cold on the hotel bed; unaware of her kiss, ripped from her soul and ordered to her lips as a final act, to bring to conclusion the hours she has spent at the window, watching his dead eyes watch the ceiling, and to give her a way to touch him beyond shutting those eyes; unaware of her eyes, at first wet, but then drying and remaining dry, even as the whimpers begin to rise from her throat, only to be lost in the din of the casino as she walks out of the hotel; unaware of her bed, the truth of her life, as it meanders back to her apartment. She undresses, brushes her teeth, lies awake in the darkness.

# the end

Photo by Joe Ansolabehere

John O'Brien was born in 1960 and
lived most of his life in California until
his death in 1994.

## A Note on the Type

This book was composed in Monotype Bodoni Book, a computer version of the typeface Bodoni. Designed in 1788 by Giambattista Bodoni, court printer to the Duke of Parma, it embodies Bodoni's ideals of a face with a modern design — flat and unbracketed serifs, decidedly thick and thin lines, and a mechanical-like form. When this face made its first appearance, printers of the day were shocked by its drastic innovation. It is today considered an outstanding type design, and is used extensively.